Miss Pickerell Harvests the Sea

MISS PICKERELL
HARVESTS THE SEA

by Ellen MacGregor and Dora Pantell

Illustrated by Charles Geer

McGRAW-HILL BOOK COMPANY

New York · Toronto · London · Sydney

Also by Ellen MacGregor
MISS PICKERELL GOES TO MARS
MISS PICKERELL AND THE GEIGER COUNTER
MISS PICKERELL GOES UNDERSEA
MISS PICKERELL GOES TO THE ARCTIC

By Ellen MacGregor and Dora Pantell
MISS PICKERELL ON THE MOON
MISS PICKERELL GOES ON A DIG

CC   9-12-10   pjv

Contents

1. Mr. Rugby Farms the Ocean 7

2. Euphus Has Some Information 18

3. Mr. Esticott Disapproves 26

4. Stir the Sea! 35

5. Another Plan 46

6. Worse, Not Better 52

7. Miss Pickerell Makes a Decision 59

8. Capsule Under the Sea 66

9. Sampling the Ocean Waters 76

10. Off the Continental Shelf 83

11. The Secret of the Bottles 93

12. On the Trail at Last 103

13. Action! Action! 111

14. Miss Pickerell Has an Idea 118

15. The Proof 126

16. Euphus Makes a Decision 136

CHAPTER ONE

Mr. Rugby Farms the Ocean

Miss Pickerell backed her automobile off the supermarket parking lot and breathed a sigh of relief.

"Well," she said, as she tucked a loose hairpin into place, made sure her eyeglasses were resting solidly on her nose, and proceeded to drive north along Main Street. "Well, thank goodness, that's over. I had no idea Square Toe City was so crowded on a weekday morning."

Miss Pickerell was talking to Pumpkins, her big black cat who sat on the front seat beside her. She patted his head and Pumpkins purred and blinked his lazy yellow eyes. Then she peered into the rearview mirror to make sure that her cow was riding comfortably in the little red trailer attached to the automobile. The trailer had a canvas awning over it to protect the cow from the sun and the rain. Miss Pickerell took good care of her animals. And she liked to take them with her when she went any-where in her automobile.

"I'll just stop by at the diner for a moment," she said, while she continued to drive slowly along in the right-hand lane. She passed the bank and the post office and the tree-shaded school that her seven nieces and nephews attended. School would be over in less than a month, she reflected.

She waited for a traffic light to change from red to orange to green. Then she went on, past the fork in the road where she ordinarily made the turn to go up to her peaceful farm on the mountain. She drove straight ahead until she reached the diner with the big, green sign in front of it, reading, MOONBURGERS, OUR SPECIALTY. M. RUGBY, PROPRIETOR. There she stopped and honked her horn.

Mr. Kettelson, the assistant proprietor, came out almost immediately. He looked even thin-ner and grayer and unhappier than usual. He carried a menu in one hand and a tray with a glass of water on it in the other, and he walked very fast.

"Oh!" he said, when he saw Miss Pickerell. "I thought you were a customer honking for curb service. That's a new idea I've put into practice since Mr. Rugby left. Or are you?"

"Am I what?" Miss Pickerell asked, trying to figure out what Mr. Kettelson was asking.

"A curb service looking for . . . I mean a customer looking for . . ."

Mr. Kettelson stopped to catch his breath.

"Excuse me, Miss Pickerell," he said, when he began talking again. "I'm very confused these days. Running the restaurant for Mr. Rugby isn't easy. And I have my own hardware shop to look in on. Of course, business there isn't very good. Still, I had to hire somebody to take care of it for me when I agreed with Mr. Rugby that I should be in charge of the diner while he . . ."

"Mr. Kettelson!" Miss Pickerell broke in, saying the words as loudly as she could. She didn't like to interrupt but she knew there was no other way. Mr. Kettelson never stopped talking when he was nervous. And he was definitely nervous this morning.

"Yes, Miss Pickerell?" Mr. Kettelson inquired, looking very surprised. "Did you want to ask me something?"

"I certainly did, Mr. Kettelson," Miss Pickerell said instantly. "I wanted to ask you for some tea. You have had your curb service for more than five weeks now and I'm perfectly familiar with it. I also wanted to ask what you have been hearing from Mr. Rugby. Have you spoken to him over the telephone lately?"

Mr. Kettleson didn't answer right away. He cleared his throat twice and drank a few sips of water from the glass on the tray each time. Then he tightened his lips and looked very disapproving.

"Mr. Rugby is a man with very strange ideas, Miss Pickerell," he said at last.

"I don't think so at all," said Miss Pickerell, coming to her friend's defense immediately.

"I have known Mr. Rugby ever since I met him in the Astral Cafeteria on the moon. Personally, I have always found his ideas very reasonable."

"I suppose you think farming the ocean is a very reasonable thing to do," Mr. Kettelson replied, sounding as though he thought exactly the opposite.

Miss Pickerell opened her mouth twice without saying anything.

"Is that what he's doing?" she asked finally.

"As if you didn't know," Mr. Kettelson said.

"Well!" Miss Pickerell exclaimed.

"I'm sorry," Mr. Kettelson apologized. "I was under the impression that Mr. Rugby told you everything."

"Mr. Rugby tells me what he chooses," Miss Pickerell said stiffly. "And I don't ask questions when he doesn't choose to tell me something."

"That's very nice of you," Mr. Kettelson said. "I admire people who mind their own business. Of course, it hasn't been my experience to know many such . . ."

Miss Pickerell didn't let him go on.

"Mr. Kettelson," she said. "Did you say something about farming an ocean?"

Mr. Kettelson transferred the menu from his left to his right hand and ran his fingers through his few gray hairs.

"Why, yes," he said. "That's what Mr. Rugby's doing in Bothomley. I think that's the name of the place on the coast where he's staying. Yes, of course it is. Anyway, as I was saying, he farms the ocean and he serves the food he grows in his new Sea Shack diner."

Miss Pickerell tried not to laugh.

"You've got it mixed up, Mr. Kettelson," she said. "Mr. Rugby is fishing the ocean, not farming it."

"I haven't got anything mixed up," Mr. Kettelson said with dignity. "Mr. Rugby is seeding a sheltered part of the sea with plankton that he takes out of the ocean. Plankton are tiny plants and animals that live at or near the surface of the ocean. The plants belong to a group called algae. Mr. Rugby and I looked it all up in the encyclopedia before he left."

"The *P* volume," Miss Pickerell said. "I know. It's my copy. I lent it to Mr. Rugby. He returned it very promptly."

"Oh?" Mr. Kettelson said. "He didn't tell me. Anyway, plankton usually stay very close to the surface at night. During the day, when the sun is very hot, these plants and animals sink a little farther down. They use the water as a protection from the intense rays of the sun."

"Yes, yes," Miss Pickerell said, "the way we use suntan lotion."

"I suppose so," Mr. Kettelson agreed. "But, as I was about to tell you, Mr. Rugby gathers them up from the ocean in a very fine net. Then he puts them into a sheltered sea nook on his sea farm. He grows mostly the plant variety."

"Plants need sunlight," Miss Pickerell stated. "They use light energy from the sun to make sugar and starch. That's how plants get their food. They make it themselves."

"I never said that they didn't," Mr. Kettelson said, sounding dignified again. "And I didn't have a chance to tell you that these algae plants look different from the plants you're used to. They're very, very small and they have no stems, no leaves, no flowers, and no roots. They multiply rapidly after Mr. Rugby transplants them to his sea farm."

"Naturally," Miss Pickerell replied. "In the ocean, they don't have as much chance to multiply. They get eaten up by the animal plankton. And the animal plankton get eaten up by larger sea creatures. They, in turn, are eaten by still larger ones. The encyclopedia calls that a food chain."

Mr. Kettelson shrugged his shoulders.

"In any case," he said, "Mr. Rugby was harvesting excellent crops until just about two weeks ago. Then everything went wrong. The small algae didn't grow well at all. And his large algae came up wilted and nearly dead."

Mr. Kettelson sighed.

"Mr. Rugby doesn't know the reason," he went on. "And he's very discouraged. He's ready to give up the whole idea. Of course, I always predicted that it wouldn't end up as a success, but . . ."

"Nonsense!" Miss Pickerell said, interrupting. "I never heard of anything more ridiculous in my life. Farming an ocean is just the same as farming a piece of land. He's probably not giving those algae the right kind of nourishment. Plants need minerals as well as sunlight. I'll just go inside and call Mr. Rugby up."

She lifted Pumpkins from her lap where he was moving round and round trying to make a comfortable place for a nap.

"You keep an eye on my animals while I talk to him, Mr. Kettelson," she said. "We'll straighten this out in no time."

"But we can't call him," Mr. Kettelson said. "He's had his number changed. It's unlisted now."

"An unlisted number in a restaurant!" Miss Pickerell said unbelievingly. "That's a very impractical idea. Why would he do that?"

Mr. Kettelson hung his head.

"I imagine it's my fault," he said. "I kept calling him too often. He told me he just couldn't stand my nagging any more."

Miss Pickerell knew exactly how Mr. Rugby felt. She was much too polite to say so, however.

"But what about his customers?" she asked instead. "What if they want to place an outgoing order? They need to know the telephone number."

"Mr. Rugby says that doesn't matter any more," Mr. Kettelson replied. "He's packing everything up and coming home."

"He can't give up that easily!" Miss Pickerell insisted. "He just can't."

Mr. Kettelson shrugged his narrow shoulders again.

Miss Pickerell looked at him and then up at the cloudless sky above. It was a beautiful day, a day for going places and doing things, she reflected, not for sitting and talking to glum Mr. Kettelson. At that moment, an idea popped into her head.

She glanced quickly at her watch.

"If I leave now," she said to Mr. Kettelson, "I can make the three o'clock train. Goodbye, Mr. Kettelson. It was nice talking to you."

She turned the ignition key and stepped on the starter.

"Wait a minute," Mr. Kettelson called through the noise of the motor. "I don't understand. The three o'clock train to where?"

"To Bothomley," Miss Pickerell called back. "To show Mr. Rugby how to farm an ocean."

"Oh!" he answered. "Would you like me to look in on your animals while you're gone?"

"I'll get my oldest niece Rosemary and my nephew Euphus to do it," Miss Pickerell replied, as she moved forward in her car. "But thanks just the same."

The noon whistle screeched from the new brassworks down the road. Miss Pickerell stepped on the accelerator and brought the speed up to her usual maximum of twenty-five miles an hour. If she hurried, she thought, she would still find Rosemary at home. For once in her life, Miss Pickerell was glad that the schools were overcrowded and that Rosemary attended morning sessions only. It was quite a way to the edge of town where her seven nieces and nephews lived, however. She could only hope that Rosemary would still be home by the time she got there.

Maybe it would be better if she called, Miss Pickerell thought as she approached a roadside telephone booth. But someone was inside talking. Someone was in the next booth that she passed, too. Miss Pickerell gave up the idea. If worse came to worse, she decided, she could explain things to their mother who would probably know where they were. Hoping with all her heart that, at least, their mother was home, Miss Pickerell stepped firmly on her accelerator, moved into the middle lane, and whizzed along as fast as her old car would let her.

CHAPTER TWO

Euphus Has Some Information

Miss Pickerell found Rosemary and Euphus waiting for her at her own farmyard gate when she drove up, tired and worried, nearly an hour later.   She was so glad to see them that she didn't even bother to ask why they hadn't taken the advice she gave them last week about having their hair cut.

"We came the minute mama gave us your message," Euphus called out to her while she was helping her cow to get off the trailer.

"We caught the bus," Rosemary added.   "It was very fast."

"I was at a meeting of the debating society," Euphus went on.   "And Rosemary had to return her overdue books to the library.   That's why we weren't home yet when you stopped. But we came right away."

"Thank you," Miss Pickerell said.   "I appreciate it."

"I'm hungry," Euphus announced. "I didn't have any lunch."

"I'll make you a chicken sandwich," Miss Pickerell promised.

"I'll make it," Rosemary said. "You'd better take that cow down into the pasture. And then you'd better start packing. You haven't got much time."

"I haven't got much to pack," Miss Pickerell answered as she went off with her cow. She led the cow past the big brown barn and across the valley to the quiet lower pasture. The cow mooed contentedly. Pumpkins, playing with stray apple tree blossoms, trotted after her.

Euphus was already eating when Miss Pickerell walked up the porch into her neat white kitchen. Rosemary was standing at the counter near the sink preparing two more sandwiches.

"They're for you," she told Miss Pickerell. "To eat on the train. And now where's your suitcase?"

"I'm not taking a suitcase," Miss Pickerell said. "I have my knitting bag."

"Oh!" Rosemary said, looking at the faded, shapeless article hanging on the doorknob. "That old thing! It's about time you got a new one."

"My knitting bag is in perfectly good condition," Miss Pickerell said. "I'll get a new one when I need it."

"All right," Rosemary answered, sighing. She moved into the hall next to the kitchen where Miss Pickerell kept her combination bureau and wardrobe closet. Miss Pickerell and Euphus followed her. Euphus carried his glass of milk along with him.

"Now what do you want to take?" Rosemary asked Miss Pickerell.

"The encyclopedia," Miss Pickerell answered her. "The *O* volume. I want to read up on ocean farms while I'm on the train."

Rosemary brought the volume in from the bedroom and put it on the horsehair sofa that stood in the hall. Miss Pickerell laid her big black umbrella alongside the book.

"Ocean farms are very important," Euphus said, as he watched. "My science teacher says they're an answer to the problem of overpopulation. Some day, there just won't be enough food from land farms to feed everyone. And, even today, in some parts of the world, people are starving because their land crops are not good."

Miss Pickerell nodded her head vigorously.

She hadn't thought of this aspect of ocean farming, but she couldn't agree more.

"And I wanted to tell you something else," Euphus continued. "There's an oceanographic institute near Bothomley. I saw a program about it on television."

"Is there really?" Miss Pickerell asked.

"I think you'd better take a sweater along," Rosemary said, opening and closing bureau drawers. "It gets cold near the ocean."

"I'll take the dark red one," Miss Pickerell said. "It's a good heavy wool."

"The pink one's prettier," Rosemary said, putting it into the knitting bag. "And it goes better with your pink voile dress."

"The television program showed how the oceanographic institute keeps in touch with the aquanauts who live at the bottom of the ocean," Euphus continued.

"Nobody can live at the bottom of the ocean," Rosemary objected.

"These aquanauts do," Euphus said. "At the bottom of this part of the ocean, anyway. They live on the sea floor under 450 feet of water and, when they leave the base, they go down in other places as far as 600 feet."

Miss Pickerell paused in her packing to stop

and think. It seemed to her that she had read somewhere that there were parts of the ocean going down to depths of 36,000 feet. Euphus was probably right, though. The depths were undoubtedly different in different places. She made a mental note to herself to look this up in the *O* volume of the encyclopedia, too. She thought she might also ask Euphus about it, but he was still talking.

"They live in a sea capsule," he was telling Rosemary. "It's 77 feet long horizontally and 18 feet in diameter and it's all dry and water-tight and air-conditioned inside. And every day the aquanauts leave the capsule to swim around for a few hours."

"What for?" Rosemary asked. "To explore?"

"Of course," Euphus answered. "So far, men have found gas and oil under the sea floor. And all sorts of metals—iron and nickel and manganese and cobalt and I forget what else."

Miss Pickerell put on her black straw hat, looked quickly in the wardrobe mirror to be certain the hat was on straight, and ran a hatpin through it to keep it firmly in place.

"I'm ready," she said, "except for the directions about Pumpkins's vitamin pills."

"I know about those," Rosemary said. "One a day, crumbled into his food."

"Very finely crumbled," Miss Pickerell warned. "He doesn't like those pills. He won't eat them if he can find some way out."

"What about the vitamin snaps?" Rosemary asked.

"They don't have as much iron in them as the pills," Miss Pickerell said. "Pumpkins needs more iron in his diet. And about the cow . . ."

"I know," Rosemary said. "I must milk her and I must talk to her."

"She's used to being talked to," Miss Pickerell reminded her niece. "She'll get very lonely if you don't do it."

"I'll talk to her," Rosemary said. "I always do."

Miss Pickerell picked up the encyclopedia and put it under her left arm. She hung her knitting bag and her big black umbrella over her left arm, too. The lunch box dangled from her right hand by a string.

"Well, that's about all," she said, taking a last look around.

"Don't worry about a thing," Rosemary reassured her.

"I'll telephone after seven," Miss Pickerell told her, "just to be sure."

She hurried down the porch steps and across the front lawn to the gate where her automobile was standing. Rosemary and Euphus dashed after her.

"I'm leaving the car at the station," she said to them. "If your older brother, Dwight, wants to use it, he can. He has my extra key."

"When will you be back, Aunt Lavinia?" Rosemary asked.

"Tomorrow," Miss Pickerell replied. "I'll let you know what time when I call tonight."

"I forgot to tell you that aquanauts communicate with the oceanographic institute by telephone," Euphus said. "And the oceanographic institute sends supplies down to them by something that works like an underwater dumbwaiter."

Miss Pickerell wished she had time to hear more about this.

"And I didn't finish telling you about the capsule the aquanauts live in," Euphus went on. "It's made of new plastic."

"Plastic!" Miss Pickerell and Rosemary exclaimed at the same time.

"Plastic," Euphus repeated, sounding very definite.

"I don't see how that's possible," Miss Pickerell said, after she had put all her belongings in the rear of the car and was settling herself in the driver's seat. "I should think they'd use heavy steel to keep all that water from coming in."

"They don't need to," Euphus said. "The capsules have enough air in them to make the pressure inside as great as the pressure of the water from outside."

Miss Pickerell thought about this as she drove down the shady road that led to the highway. She remembered the houses on the moon and how they, too, needed an artificial atmosphere. Both out in space and underwater there was not enough natural air for people to breathe.

Well, on this trip, Miss Pickerell said to herself confidently, she wasn't going to be troubled by any such problems. She was going to stay overnight in an ordinary country motel. She was going to help Mr. Rugby with something as simple as basic instruction in farming. Why, it would be like having a nice little vacation. She hadn't had a vacation in years. Miss Pickerell smiled as she made the turn onto the main road and drove along toward the station ahead.

CHAPTER THREE

Mr. Esticott Disapproves

It was eighteen minutes to three when Miss
Pickerell got to the station. That gave her
plenty of time to go into the telegraph office and
send Mr. Rugby a wire. She told him the exact
time the train would arrive in Bothomley and
asked him to meet her. Next, she walked over
to the ticket window. Five women were lined
up in front of it. Miss Pickerell thought they
all looked like ladies who might ask the ticket
seller a lot of questions.

"I'd better not take any chances," Miss Pickerell said to herself as she glanced up at the big
station clock. "I'll buy my ticket on the
train."

The day-coach car that she entered was nearly
empty. Miss Pickerell made herself comfortable on a green plush seat next to a window.
First, she placed her umbrella, her knitting
bag, and the encyclopedia on an adjoining va-
cant seat. Then she opened her lunch box.

Rosemary had wrapped the sandwiches carefully in wax paper. She had put in some salt and pepper and a little jar of mayonnaise, too. There was also a shiny red apple partly covered with a paper napkin in a corner of the lunch box.

Miss Pickerell decided she would read while she ate her lunch. She opened the *O* volume of the encyclopedia to the section on oceanography. She soon became so interested that she didn't even notice when the train started moving.

She was just reading the part about manganese and phosphates and other valuable chemicals that lie on the bottom of the sea, and finishing her first chicken sandwich, when Mr. Esticott walked in from the car ahead. He was wearing his navy blue uniform with the gold buttons on it and his conductor's cap. The jacket of his uniform was much too tight across the stomach. Two of the buttons looked as though they might pop open any second. Miss Pickerell was very surprised to see him.

"Why, Mr. Esticott!" she exclaimed. "What are you doing here? I'm sure you haven't been demoted from the baggage master's job you've been performing so excellently."

"Not at all, Miss Pickerell," Mr. Esticott replied, sounding very insulted at even the suspicion of such an idea. "This is my day off."

Miss Pickerell didn't fully understand. Mr. Esticott always worked behind the soda fountain in the Square Toe City drugstore on his day off. He made the most delicious peppermint ice cream sodas. Miss Pickerell loved peppermint. Her mouth watered just thinking about those sodas.

"I got a little tired of the soda-fountain business," Mr. Esticott said, understanding why Miss Pickerell looked puzzled and trying to explain. "Travelling on the train makes a little change."

"Change is always nice," Miss Pickerell agreed. Privately, she couldn't see much change involved in riding back and forth on the same train route once a week, but she didn't like to say so.

"Where are you off to, Miss Pickerell?" Mr. Esticott asked her.

"To Bothomley," Miss Pickerell said, handing him a crisp $10 bill.

"Bothomley," Mr. Esticott repeated, as he thumbed through the train schedule he took out of an inside pocket. "Let's see now. That will cost you $5.48. Plus tax."

He carefully counted out the change for Miss Pickerell. Then he punched a ticket for her and slid it into place on the back of the seat in front of her own.

"What are you going to do in Bothomley?" he asked.

"I'm going to visit Mr. Rugby," Miss Pickerell told him.

Mr. Esticott coughed. He said "Hmmm" several times.

"Did you want to say something to me, Mr. Esticott?" Miss Pickerell asked.

Mr. Esticott sighed. He turned to collect tickets from two people across the aisle. Then he turned back to Miss Pickerell.

"I hope you won't mind my telling you this," he said to Miss Pickerell. "But I know what Mr. Rugby is doing in Bothomley. And I don't think you should be going there to join him."

"Well!" Miss Pickerell spluttered, wondering why Mr. Esticott considered it his business to approve or disapprove of her errands. "I must say . . ."

"It's all very unnecessary," Mr. Esticott went on. "This interest of Mr. Rugby's in oceans, I mean."

"Everyone should be interested in oceans," Miss Pickerell retorted. "Why, the ocean is the largest single feature of the earth's surface. Oceanic waters cover almost 61 percent of the northern hemisphere and more than 80 percent of the southern hemisphere. It says so right here in the encyclopedia."

Mr. Esticott leaned down to look more closely at the page Miss Pickerell was showing him.

"That's a very interesting picture," he said, pointing to a bright red and black illustration on the same page. "The man is growing sea plants on bamboo poles, isn't he?"

"Poles sunk in the muddy bottoms of shallow bays," Miss Pickerell said. "That's one kind of ocean farm. Mr. Rugby has a different kind."

"I know," Mr. Esticott said sadly. "Mr. Kettelson explained the whole thing to me."

"By farming the ocean, Mr. Rugby is doing the world a great service," Miss Pickerell went on, trying hard to make Mr. Esticott understand. "My middle nephew, Euphus, explained it all to me while I was packing and I . . ."

"Both Mr. Kettelson and I are of the opinion

that Mr. Rugby should give up the ocean farm," Mr. Esticott interrupted.

Miss Pickerell sat bolt upright with indignation.

"Mr. Kettelson and I happen to see eye to eye in this particular respect," Mr. Esticott continued. "We are both men who don't like dangerous undertakings."

"There's nothing dangerous about ocean farming," Miss Pickerell said. "Nothing dangerous at all. If there were, this encyclopedia would say something about it."

Mr. Esticott coughed and said "Hmmm" again.

"Yes, Mr. Esticott?" Miss Pickerell asked.

"I don't like to be the one to call this to your attention, Miss Pickerell," Mr. Esticott said, "but your encyclopedia is nearly three years and four months old. I remember the day you bought it. It was exactly one week after my daughter who lives in Plentibush City got married. Naturally . . ."

"I don't see what she has to do with this," Miss Pickerell interrupted.

"Oh, it isn't that she has anything to do with it," Mr. Esticott explained. "It's just that your encyclopedia is out of date. Things happen so fast these days, encyclopedias can't keep up with them."

Miss Pickerell had to agree that this was true.

"And you don't read the newspapers as thoroughly as I do," Mr. Esticott hinted.

"Exactly what dangers did you read about in the newspapers?" Miss Pickerell asked, almost afraid to hear the answer.

"Oh," Mr. Esticott said, taking his time about replying. "It isn't any special danger that I had in mind. I was just thinking that in an enterprise as new as ocean farming, one can expect almost anything."

Miss Pickerell stared at him. She could hardly believe her ears. Why, he was trying to frighten her about things that might not even exist!

"It's because I consider myself your friend that I'm telling you this, Miss Pickerell," Mr. Esticott added, sounding a little embarrassed. "In my opinion, you have already gotten yourself mixed up in enough adventures."

He looked out of the window at the station they were passing.

"I'm afraid I have to go now," he said. "I

have to collect the tickets in the next car. And in a few minutes, I have to announce the name of the station we'll be pulling into."

"Yes, of course," Miss Pickerell said, turning back to her encyclopedia. But she could no longer concentrate on reading. She was sorry she hadn't brought her knitting along. It would have helped take her mind off Mr. Esticott and his silly, nameless fears. Miss Pickerell liked to know about things definitely. She liked to plan whatever needed to be done.

She sighed. She wished the train would move faster. She wished she were in Bothomley with Mr. Rugby this very minute. Mr. Rugby always looked so certain and cheerful and jolly, no matter what was about to happen.

CHAPTER FOUR

Stir the Sea!

Mr. Rugby didn't look the least bit jolly when Miss Pickerell spotted him standing near the information desk in the Bothomley station. His round face was long now and his bouncing double chins seemed settled in a permanent sagging position. He was very sun-tanned, but Miss Pickerell noticed the rings under his eyes that the tan couldn't hide and she saw the strain around his mouth when he tried to smile.

"I'm so very glad to see you, Miss Pickerell," Mr. Rugby said, as he ran toward her in his old enthusiastic way. "I hope you had a nice journey."

"I read most of the way," Miss Pickerell said, trying to forget Mr. Esticott and his gloomy forebodings. "About ocean farms. They're very important."

Mr. Rugby beamed. Miss Pickerell remembered that he was very easily encouraged.

"My truck's in front of the station," he said, taking Miss Pickerell's knitting bag from her. "I'll drive you to your motel."

"I'd rather see the farm first," said Miss

Pickerell. "There's still enough light for me to get a good look."

Mr. Rugby quickly led the way to the truck.

Miss Pickerell could smell the ocean as soon as Mr. Rugby drove away from the station. It was a fresh, healthy smell and it made her feel very energetic.

"How far away is the farm, Mr. Rugby?" she asked.

"We drive through the town," Mr. Rugby explained. "Then we climb a few hills. The farm's on the sea coast on the bottom of the other side of the hills."

A moment later, Mr. Rugby steered his truck into Bothomley's main street.

"Oh!" said Miss Pickerell when she saw the Sea Shack on the corner they were slowly approaching. She recognized it immediately. There were three blue-green jars in the top part of the window. They reminded her of the colored jars in a comfortable, old-fashioned drugstore. But these jars were clearly labelled SEA WATER. And the words, HAVE SEA FUN ON A HOT BUN IN THE SEA SHACK RESTAURANT were printed below them. Above them, a very neat sign displayed the name M. RUGBY in white letters on a speckled-green background. The name was repeated on the green blinds drawn behind the plate-glass door and the window.

"It's the finest shop on the block, Mr. Rugby," she said, admiringly.

"It's closed," Mr. Rugby said sadly. "I don't have enough food to keep it open."

"We'll have to do something about that," Miss Pickerell replied with unmistakable decision. "Where's the farm?"

"We can see it from the top of the last hill," Mr. Rugby said. "I'll take a shortcut."

Miss Pickerell sighed. She knew all about Mr. Rugby's preference for shortcuts. But whenever he tried them, they somehow never ended up as short.

Mr. Rugby pressed his foot down on the gas pedal. They drove quickly to the end of the main street and then up a steep country road. They climbed and climbed for what seemed like forever. Miss Pickerell was just about to ask whether they were getting any nearer when they reached the top of a hill and began to descend. Miss Pickerell leaned forward. She gasped. It was all so totally different from anything she had expected.

Mr. Rugby's farm began at the water's edge with several large rocks where something resembling seaweed lay spread out to dry. Miss Pickerell wasn't entirely sure. She had never seen seaweed in so many sizes and in such brilliant colors before. To the right of the rocks, the land curved in and around to form a cove almost surrounded by stones on the ocean side. Directly in front of the rocks with the seaweed, a wooden dock extended at least one hundred feet over the ocean. Two long poles stood upright at the far end of the dock. A number of finely-meshed, cone-shaped nets hung on one of

the poles. Two rowboats lay tied up to the other. More poles with ropes attached to them stuck out from both sides of the dock.

The truck was practically at the water's edge by now. Mr. Rugby stopped with a sharp jerk and hurried to help Miss Pickerell out. She looked to the right and to the left of her. She didn't know what to examine first.

"That's seaweed," Mr. Rugby said, pointing to the colorful tangle of plants on the rocks and making it unnecessary for Miss Pickerell to ask. "I serve the green and purple variety as a salad, the blue-green in a relish, and the brown kind as a filler for pancakes. After I clean and dry it all, of course."

"Of course," Miss Pickerell repeated mechanically, while she moved away from the rocks to walk out on the dock. Mr. Rugby talked all the way.

"For transporting the crops back to the restaurant," he explained, as they passed a number of barrels and bins standing on the dock. Miss Pickerell nodded.

"For collecting the plankton," he said, as she approached the nets. "My helper and I go out in the rowboats. We gather the plankton in the nets and then we transfer some of them to the cove back there. It's a naturally sheltered cove because it has those stones almost all around it."

"Yes," said Miss Pickerell, moving now to one side of the dock to study some very odd plants she saw suspended in the water there. They looked as though they were being cultivated on the ropes that hung down in the water.

"My kelp beds," Mr. Rugby said mournfully. "They were growing very well until recently. Now . . ."

He pulled one of the ropes up so that Miss Pickerell could get a better look. She saw that most of the plants were withered.

"My rockweeds over there are failing, too," he said, pointing to the other side of the dock and sighing deeply.

Miss Pickerell noticed that Mr. Rugby had his various crops as carefully separated on his sea farm as she did her own beans and tomatoes in Square Toe County. She admired the orderly arrangement.

"I read somewhere that there are at least ten thousand species of algae living in sea water," Miss Pickerell told him.

Mr. Rugby nodded.

"Here, I want you to look at this, Miss Pickerell," he said proudly.

He handed her a folded-over piece of speckled-green cardboard that he took out of his jacket pocket. It was a menu, shaped like a fish. Planktonburgers on soft buns were featured as an entree. Miss Pickerell spent a minute inspecting the list of prices. They seemed very reasonable.

"But I have almost no more plankton left," Mr. Rugby said, taking the menu from Miss Pickerell and gazing at it sadly. "Come, I'll show you where I grow them."

He led Miss Pickerell back toward the cove at the land end of the dock. At first, the water there looked to her like a lush green meadow just under the surface of the ocean. When she got nearer, Miss Pickerell decided it looked more like a murky, greenish soup. When she stood very close, she saw it was a very uneven soup. In some places, it was good and thick. In other places, it was so thin that all she could see was blue, clear water.

"Those are the *diatoms*," Mr. Rugby said, pointing to the soupy water. "They're the smallest and the most numerous plants of the plankton. They can't swim. They just float. They have two shells that fit together like a little box. I've seen pictures taken of them through a microscope that show . . ."

Miss Pickerell was no longer listening. She had read every word that Mr. Rugby was telling her while she was on the train, and she had seen the exact same pictures. She kept looking indignantly at the uneven appearance of the water in the ocean cove.

"Why, my oldest niece, Rosemary, could make a better soup than that," she exclaimed.

"Soup?" Mr. Rugby repeated questioningly, trying to keep up with what Miss Pickerell was saying.

"But if my niece, Rosemary, were making that soup," Miss Pickerell went on, "she'd give it a good stir. She'd see to it that all the vegetables and the spices were thoroughly mixed with the water. My oldest niece, Rosemary, knows . . ."

Miss Pickerell stopped suddenly. An idea was beginning to take shape in her head.

"Forevermore!" she breathed. "It's really very simple."

Mr. Rugby stared.

"Yes," Miss Pickerell said, firmly and decisively. "What you have to do, Mr. Rugby, is to stir the sea!"

Mr. Rugby was speechless.

Miss Pickerell reflected that she had never known Mr. Rugby to be at a loss for words before. She took a strong hold on herself and tried to explain.

"It's like sugar in a cup of tea," she said. "You have to stir it, if you want your tea to taste sweet."

Now, Mr. Rugby looked dumbfounded.

Miss Pickerell decided to start from the beginning.

"Mr. Rugby," she said, speaking slowly so that Mr. Rugby would follow her meaning, "plants need minerals as well as sunlight. Your plants depend on the minerals at the bottom of the ocean to help nourish them. Ocean currents stir up the ocean and carry the phosphates and the nitrates up to them."

"Oh!" Mr. Rugby said.

"Maybe the currents have not been strong

enough to bring nourishment up for all your plants," Miss Pickerell continued. "That would explain why some of them are wilted and, also, why so many of the plankton have died and sunk down to the bottom of the ocean. It could explain why you have patches like deserts in your meadow of diatoms."

Mr. Rugby nodded his head several times to show that he understood.

"But . . . but," he asked breathlessly. "What do we do now?"

"We stir the waters of your ocean farm," Miss Pickerell said, unhesitatingly. "We stir it with a giant spoon."

Mr. Rugby wiped his perspiring forehead with his big white handkerchief.

"With WHAT?" he asked uneasily.

"There IS such a spoon," Miss Pickerell stated, not intending to be put off by Mr. Rugby's ignorance. "Well, maybe not exactly a spoon. It's really a huge chain with metal flaps in its links that is anchored on the bottom. The deep ocean currents cause the bottom flaps to move. And the movement continues from link to link, on up to the top of the chain. It's a vertical movement, from bottom to top. I saw a movie about it once."

Mr. Rugby stared with open admiration. When he looked away, Miss Pickerell knew what he was thinking. She was wondering about it herself. Where were they going to get this vertical mixer? And who was going to anchor it for them at the bottom of the ocean? Actually, she had an idea. But she was almost afraid to tell Mr. Rugby about it. He became enthusiastic so quickly. What if the idea turned out to be useless? She decided to take a chance.

Mr. Rugby . . ." she said, still hesitating a little.

"Yes, Miss Pickerell?" Mr. Rugby replied instantly.

"Did you know there was an oceanographic institute in Bothomley?" she asked.

Mr. Rugby knew immediately what she meant.

"It's only a few miles from here," he said, beaming broadly. "We'll go there right away."

"We must be very sensible about this," Miss Pickerell warned. "We really don't know what we can expect . . ."

But she ran in the direction of the truck. Mr. Rugby, panting a little, followed. He helped her take the high step up to her seat.

CHAPTER FIVE

Another Plan

It was half past six when Miss Pickerell and Mr. Rugby walked up the gravel path that led to the front door of the oceanographic institute. At precisely the same second that Miss Pickerell put her finger on the buzzer, the one light in the long yellow building went out.

"They're closed," Mr. Rugby said dully. "We're too late."

"Not at all," Miss Pickerell replied, adjusting her hat, which had slipped a little to one side during the truck ride. "If someone has just put out the light, someone is still inside. That's the person we'll see."

Footsteps sounded in the quiet building. They echoed as they came closer to the door. A hand fumbled with the latch on the other side.

The tall, sandy-haired young man who pulled the door open looked at them curiously.

"Yes?" he asked in a quiet, pleasant voice, as he switched on some lights.

Miss Pickerell wasn't quite sure how she ought to explain. She hadn't really had a chance to organize her thinking.

"Are . . . are you an oceanographer?" she asked because she couldn't think of another way to begin.

The young man laughed, showing two dimples in his cheeks.

"I guess so," he said. "Sort of a junior variety."

Miss Pickerell laughed, too. It was easy to talk to this very relaxed young man.

"We have something important to ask you," she said. "May we come in?"

The young man showed them into a small entrance hall. It smelled strongly of lemon furniture polish. Whoever attended to domestic duties in this place, Miss Pickerell reflected, knew how to keep a house.

She and Mr. Rugby followed the young man through the entrance hall, then down a long corridor with closed doors on either side, and finally into a room that seemed to be a combined office and laboratory. Miss Pickerell counted three telephones, four filing cabinets, and two desks. A large binocular microscope stood on one corner of each of the desks. A half-open closet revealed scuba breathing apparatus and diving suits on hangers.

"My name's Peters," the young man said, as he pulled out a chair for Miss Pickerell to sit on and indicated another one for Mr. Rugby. "Most people call me Pete."

"I'm Miss Pickerell and this is my friend, Mr. Rugby," Miss Pickerell answered. "Mr. Rugby has an ocean farm."

"Oh!" Pete said, his brown eyes lighting up. "That's my specialty. I have a tagged specimen of a sea plant on the slide of my microscope right now."

Mr. Rugby and Miss Pickerell exchanged encouraging glances.

"My colleague, Rube, who sits at the other desk," Pete added, "is more interested in rocks. We get all kinds of rocks sent up to us for examination. The ocean floor has many interesting examples."

"Oh!" Miss Pickerell breathed, wondering whether she would ever have a chance to see some of them. She loved rocks. She herself had a whole collection that the Governor was always borrowing to exhibit at state fairs. With an effort, she brought her thoughts back to the ocean farm.

"Mr. Rugby's crops have not been doing very well recently," she went on. "We believe it's because they're not getting enough nourishment from the bottom of the ocean."

"Bravo, Miss Pickerell!" Pete said. "That's exactly my theory about the requirements of ocean farms. There needs to be an upwelling of water to bring the minerals up to the crops."

Mr. Rugby beamed at Miss Pickerell.

"And we could bring about this upwelling with a vertical mixer," Miss Pickerell continued. "A chain with metal flaps."

"Right again," Pete said. "Or with a long plastic pipe through which the water from the bottom is pumped up. Both methods are very effective."

He paused to give Miss Pickerell a congratulatory smile.

"But we gave up using the chain and the pump a long time ago," he added. "We don't even have that type of equipment any more."

Miss Pickerell felt her heart sink down to her toes. She was afraid even to glance in Mr. Rugby's direction. She couldn't bear to see the look of disappointment on his face.

"We have something more modern now," Pete said proudly.

Miss Pickerell held her breath. She looked quickly at Mr. Rugby. He seemed to be almost choking with impatience.

"We use a nuclear reactor," Pete said. "When atoms are split in reactors, much heat is produced. And what happens?"

Miss Pickerell was about to try to answer but Pete went on without waiting.

"It's really very simple," he said. "What happens is exactly what takes place in a hot water heating system. The hot water is less dense. It weighs less than the cold water in the system. The cold water moves down and pushes the hot water up. And in the ocean, when the warm water moves up from the bottom, it carries minerals along with it to the plants on top."

Miss Pickerell released her breath in a great sigh of relief.

"Could we . . . Might we . . . ?" she began.

"Sure, Miss Pickerell," said Pete, reading her mind quickly and correctly. "I'll ask the boys at the bottom to get the nuclear reactor going for you. I'll give them a call. That's easy. We have two-way underwater telephones. By tomorrow morning, Mr. Rugby, your farm will most probably be fine again."

Miss Pickerell and Mr. Rugby walked back to the truck in almost total silence. Miss Pickerell was too tired to speak. Mr. Rugby made a number of attempts but they all seemed to end up as gasps.

"I can hardly wait till tomorrow," he said at last, when he started the truck rolling.

"Neither can I," said Miss Pickerell, holding on to her hat and thinking that she must call Rosemary even before she and Mr. Rugby sat down to have some dinner.

CHAPTER SIX

Worse, Not Better

Miss Pickerell got up early the next morning. Looking out of her motel-room window, she saw that Mr. Rugby's truck had not yet arrived. She felt much too anxious to sit still, and walked up and down the red-carpeted room.

"I won't wait," she told herself, coming to a decision. "I know the way to the sea farm. I'll just walk over there by myself."

Before she left the room, she made sure that she had a handkerchief, her extra pair of glasses in her knitting bag, and her umbrella just in case it might rain. She locked the door carefully and walked toward the dining room.

"I'll give Mr. Rugby another half-hour to get here," she reasoned. "I can have breakfast while I'm waiting."

It was only seven, but the dining room was already crowded. A waitress in a green and white polka-dot uniform asked Miss Pickerell whether she minded sharing a table. Miss Pickerell did mind but she couldn't very well say so. The waitress seated her next to a red-faced, military-looking gentlemen who introduced himself immediately.

"Lieutenant Commander S. S. Cripes, U.S. Navy, retired," he said. "Lovely weather we're having."

Miss Pickerell agreed.

"Nice day to take a stroll along the ocean," Lieutenant Commander Cripes went on. "I wish I had the time. But I'm on a special assignment right now. Always, always, too much to do!"

Miss Pickerell wondered what the lieutenant commander had to do in this small seaside town, but she felt it would be impolite to ask. She said nothing.

Lieutenant Commander Cripes didn't seem to expect an answer. He went right on talking.

"When I was with the Navy," he said, "I was always sent out on special assignments. You see, I was with the Personnel Department and problems were always coming up. I remember once I was sent to . . ."

Miss Pickerell stopped listening. She drank her orange juice and pursued her own thoughts. From time to time, when the lieutenant commander looked at her questioningly, she nodded and hoped she was supplying the proper response. But mostly, she kept her mind on Mr. Rugby and his ocean farm.

It was when Miss Pickerell was finishing her large cup of tea with milk in it that she saw the truck approaching the motel. She put the cup down instantly.

"Excuse me, Lieutenant Commander," she said, the first second he stopped between sentences. "My friend, Mr. Rugby, is here. We have to go look at his ocean farm."

"Ocean farm!" the lieutenant commander exclaimed. "I . . ."

But Miss Pickerell did not wait for him to finish. She rushed to the man at the cash register to hand him her bill with her signature and room number on it, and ran out to meet Mr. Rugby.

The moment she saw his face, she knew something was wrong. Mr. Rugby did not keep her in suspense.

"It's worse, not better!" he said, as he brought the truck to a screeching halt.

Miss Pickerell was stunned.

"I went to look," Mr. Rugby went on. "The minute I got up. I couldn't bear to wait. And I . . ."

"Yes, yes," Miss Pickerell said, eager to get to the point. "What is the farm like?"

Mr. Rugby threw out his hands in a gesture of despair.

"*Everything* is wilted now," he said mournfully.

Miss Pickerell took a few minutes to think about this.

"Maybe you went too soon, Mr. Rugby," she suggested, though she didn't really believe it. "Maybe it all looks better by now."

Mr. Rugby brightened immediately.

"Should we go see?" he asked.

He leaned over and practically lifted Miss Pickerell into the truck. He drove so fast, that they were at the ocean farm before Miss Pickerell even had a chance to caution him about being careful around the curves. She saw right away that the crops were worse. She didn't even have to get out of the truck to take a closer look. Nearly all the plankton had sunk far below the surface. And the kelp on the ropes sagged lifelessly in the clear ocean water.

"What do we do now?" Mr. Rugby pleaded.

"Go back to the institute," Miss Pickerell said, taking a firm grip on her resolution to get to the bottom of this mystery. Her theory about stirring the sea was right. She was sure of it. Something else was going on, something she couldn't understand at all.

"It wouldn't surprise me if that nuclear reactor was out of order," she added.

Mr. Rugby put his foot on the gas pedal.

They met Pete just as they were rolling up to the institute. He was coming from the direction of the ocean.

"We have some very important company," he called, as he walked over to them. "A specialist has come to help us with our underseas personnel problems. I've just sent him down in our undersea elevator."

"Undersea elevator?" Mr. Rugby asked.

Pete answered Mr. Rugby's question.

"The undersea elevator is what we use to get down to our undersea quarters, Mr. Rugby," he explained. "And up again, of course. It's like an automatic elevator. But when you ride down in it, you breathe a changing mixture of helium and oxygen to get your body accustomed to the undersea environment."

"Where is it?" Mr. Rugby asked, looking around for the elevator.

"Oh, attached to the top of one of our underseas capsules," Pete explained. "We leave it there for the men to use when they want to come up."

"About the ocean farm," Miss Pickerell said, changing the subject, "what did . . ."

"That reminds me!" Pete burst out. "I spoke yesterday to Captain Bean, our underwater executive officer. He said he'd be glad to start the nuclear reactor for you. He said it would take his mind off his personnel problems and that was wonderful. So . . ."

Miss Pickerell's face fell.

Mr. Rugby began wringing his hands.

Pete stared, mystified.

"Is anything the matter?" he asked, looking at them.

Miss Pickerell found her voice first.

"The farm's much worse," she said, summing it all up.

"Impossible!" Pete said instantly. " I know my marine biology. It couldn't have happened that way."

Miss Pickerell said that she agreed with him completely but the condition of the plants was beyond dispute. Mr. Rugby described the plants. Pete scratched his head.

"Captain Bean is a very reliable man," he said finally. "Still, anything can happen. Maybe he forgot about the reactor. Maybe he had another personnel problem. I can find out. I can telephone . . ."

He began walking quickly up the gravel path.

Miss Pickerell, using her umbrella to lean on, jumped out of the truck to run after him. Mr. Rugby, panting again, followed.

"Better wait in the entrance hall," Pete said, when they reached the door. "It's really against the rules to have visitors in our workrooms. And . . ."

"Rules should be obeyed," Miss Pickerell said, nodding.

"I'll be back in five minutes," Pete promised, as he raced down the corridor.

CHAPTER SEVEN

Miss Pickerell Makes a Decision

Pete returned in less than five minutes. He looked anything but relaxed.

Miss Pickerell got the point at once.

"The captain *did* get the nuclear reactor going," she said flatly.

Pete nodded. Miss Pickerell sighed. Mr. Rugby clenched his hands and looked up at the sky.

"Captain Bean *agrees* that it shouldn't have happened this way," Pete said.

Miss Pickerell found this encouraging.

"Well, then," she began, "he should . . ."

"He won't," Pete interrupted. "He says he can't be bothered with ocean farms. Not at the moment. Maybe never. He's in a terrible mood."

"Oh?" Miss Pickerell asked.

"It's that personnel specialist," Pete explained. "He's making the captain write out reports about everything and everybody. In quadruplicate."

Miss Pickerell didn't see exactly how this

would help with the personnel problems, whatever they were. She decided not to ask Pete
about them. She didn't think now was the time
for her to pursue the subject.

"There must be *something* we can do," she
said grimly.

"What did you have in mind?" Pete asked.

"Nothing yet," Miss Pickerell admitted. "I
have to think about it. But I know one thing.
We won't ever find out why the farm got worse
if we just stand around here."

She walked over to the window and looked
out at the ocean. It was a peaceful scene. At
this hour of the morning, the water looked blue
and very gentle. Two men in work clothes
were quietly raking some leaves from the dirt
road that led down to the sea front. The sea
front itself was deserted except for a long gray
barge that lay anchored there. The barge had
the words OCEANOGRAPHIC INSTITUTE
clearly lettered in white paint on both sides.

"What do you use that barge for?" Miss
Pickerell asked Pete.

"To get out to the places in the ocean where
the elevators come up," Pete answered, joining
her at the window.

"Oh!" Miss Pickerell said, suddenly struck by what Pete was saying. An idea was coming into her head. At the very same instant, she suddenly saw Mr. Esticott's face clearly in front of her. She could almost hear him, too. He was uttering his usual preliminary cough and saying, "You have already gotten yourself mixed up in enough adventures, Miss Pickerell." Miss Pickerell's heart thumped wildly. She resolutely put the image of Mr. Esticott out of her mind.

"How often do these elevators come up to the surface?" she asked.

"Why, as often as we need them, Miss Pickerell," Pete said. "We just telephone and . . ."

He halted abruptly. Miss Pickerell had the feeling that he was reading her mind again. She was right.

"No!" he said. "That's impossible! You can't go down in the undersea elevator!"

"Why not?" Miss Pickerell asked, surprised. It seemed to her the only sensible thing to do at this time. How else could she find out why the underwater stirring had made the sea farm worse?

"A million reasons," Pete said, excitedly.

"The first one is that my chief wouldn't like it."

"I'll go talk to him," Miss Pickerell said, touching her hair in the back to make sure that the pins were neatly in place.

"You can't," Pete said. "He's underseas with that personnel man."

"Then I can ask him once I'm down there," Miss Pickerell replied. "If he doesn't approve, I can always come up again."

"That sounds reasonable," Mr. Rugby commented, nodding.

"But you don't understand," Pete said, pacing back and forth and looking very exasperated. "This is a trip to the bottom of the ocean. The bottom on the continental shelf where you want to go is about 500 feet down. The pressure of the water there is crushing, almost sixteen times what it is at sea level."

Miss Pickerell's patience was beginning to wear thin. She stood up very erect and planted herself firmly in front of Pete.

"I remember distinctly," she said, "that you told me the elevator was filled with a changing mixture of oxygen and helium so that people travelling down could get comfortably adjusted to the undersea environment. I understand fully that the farther down people go, the more gas pressure they need inside their bodies to balance the increasing pressure of the water. I don't completely understand about the helium, but I suppose I can find out."

"I can tell you that," Pete said. "There is actually four times as much nitrogen in the air as oxygen."

"We were talking about helium," Miss Pickerell said. "I know about the nitrogen."

"Well," Pete said, "we used to mix the nitrogen in with the oxygen. But we don't any more. We use helium instead. That's because nitrogen does funny things to people. It makes them overconfident, and worse, forget where they are."

"That can be very dangerous," Mr. Rugby said.

"Helium also reduces some of the danger of getting the bends," Pete went on.

"The bends?" Mr. Rugby asked. "I haven't heard about those."

"We needn't discuss them now," Miss Pickerell said, going back to the subject of getting down to the bottom of the ocean. "I assume the underseas living quarters and the sea labs are very carefully pressurized."

"Of course," Pete replied.

"Then there's no problem," Miss Pickerell decided. "Do we need any scuba equipment?"

"Not on the way down," Pete said. "But when people leave the pressurized elevator, they have to swim to the hatch of the capsule. The hatch is the entrance to the capsule."

"I'm a very good swimmer," Miss Pickerell said.

"It's a pity they don't have a plastic canopy opening up to cover the way to the hatch," Mr. Rugby said. "Airplane companies provide a canopy. To protect passengers against bad weather. Why, Miss Pickerell even has a canopy for her cow."

Miss Pickerell winced. She wished Mr. Rugby hadn't brought up the subject of her cow just now. She wished she were home with her cow and her cat right this minute instead of embarking on a voyage to the bottom of the sea.

"It won't take too long," she told herself comfortingly. "I'll just find out what's wrong and then I'll come up again. I may even take a late train home tonight."

She turned to Pete.

"I'm ready," she said. "I'm ready to go down. What about you, Mr. Rugby?"

"Any time, Miss Pickerell," Mr. Rugby said.

"Oh, no!" Pete exclaimed. "Not two of you! One is bad enough, but two . . ."

"Very well," Miss Pickerell replied. "I'll go alone. Mr. Rugby will wait here."

Pete still hesitated.

"There's one more thing, Miss Pickerell," he said. "You can't go without an institute staff member. It's against regulations. I'd have to go with you."

Miss Pickerell took a quick look at Pete's bright, shining eyes. She could tell that he wanted very much to go down and try to unravel the mystery of his marine biology.

"How soon can you be ready?" she asked.

"Oh, right away," Pete said at once. "All I have to do is get the scuba equipment and telephone for the . . ." He started to run.

Miss Pickerell could no longer hear him. She had stepped outside through the front door. It had grown very windy. Maybe it was going to rain after all, she thought. She threw her pink sweater over her shoulders. She clutched her knitting bag tightly in one hand and her umbrella in the other, as she walked slowly down to the barge.

CHAPTER EIGHT

Capsule Under the Sea

So as not to waste even a minute in the elevator, Miss Pickerell changed into her rubber diving suit in the rest room on the barge. She also put on her rubber flippers, her windowed mask, and her pressure tank.

"Good!" Pete said, as he helped her climb down from the barge on to a ladder in the decompression chamber. He held her hand while she took the last step down the ladder. Then he guided her past a boxed-off corner that accommodated a large panel of instruments and across the room to a window with glass at least twelve inches thick.

"It's a short ride," he told her. "We're going down less than five hundred feet."

Miss Pickerell's heart thumped so loudly, she was sure Pete could hear it. She looked around for a place to sit. There was only a foam-rubber cushion on the floor. She decided to stand.

"We're off," Pete shouted, as the elevator slipped suddenly and noiselessly beneath the waves.

They kept going down, down, down. Miss Pickerell could hardly bear it. To calm herself, she concentrated on peering out of the glass window. She watched goggle-eyed fish of all shapes and sizes swimming past her. She saw clouds of plankton floating by. They sparkled like jewels in the blue-green light. But the light was growing dimmer with every yard of depth. Dimmer and dimmer and . . .

"We're almost there," Pete said. "I'll go and change."

"Mercy!" Miss Pickerell breathed in the dark.

The elevator came to a hissing stop. High-intensity lamps on the outside of the elevator suddenly lit up the waters.

"We dive now," Pete, once more beside her, announced. "Right through the hatch!"

Miss Pickerell watched some boards near her feet open up. She closed her eyes. Pete checked her pressure tank.

"All set," he said. "Follow me. Ready! Go!"

Miss Pickerell stood on the edge in diving position. She put her mouthpiece in place, counted to ten, and plunged.

She felt nothing, not even the icy numbness

she had expected. Then she remembered that her rubber suit insulated her against some of the cold. She relaxed. She wished she had time to examine more closely the large unfamiliar fish that swam quietly along with her and some of the strange red plants that she passed. But she knew she had to keep her eyes on Pete. He was moving rapidly toward the end of the lamp-lit area. He was starting to climb now and gesturing for her to join him. Her extended hands touched the rung of a ladder. She followed Pete up, rung by rung, through another open hatch which she saw was the entrance to an underwater capsule. She didn't

have a chance to notice more than its cigar-like shape and the regularly-spaced port-hole windows across its length.

Pete stood up, removed his mask, shook water off his flippers, and walked into a lighted room. Miss Pickerell did the same.

"Who's there?" a falsetto voice screamed out

at her. Miss Pickerell stood stockstill and stared. The high, duck-like sounds were coming out of the mouth of a stocky, square-jawed man sitting at a desk in the middle of the room. He did not even look up. He clicked four sheets of paper and carbon into a typewriter, banged the keys furiously, and again quacked, "Who's there?"

"It's the helium," Pete whispered, grinning and sounding even more like a duck than the man at the typewriter. "It does that to the voice. We usually have a helium speech converter around that makes us sound a little better. It's out of order."

"Everything's out of order," the man said, suddenly sitting forward and fixing his bright blue eyes on Miss Pickerell. "What are you doing here?"

Miss Pickerell automatically looked around for a door that she might close. If they were going to have an argument, it seemed to her they ought to have a little more privacy. Personally, she was boiling inside. She had come down here for a perfectly good reason and she had every intention of making that clear to the man behind the typewriter.

"There is no door," he said, watching her.

"We don't need it. The water can't come in here any more than it could enter a drinking glass that was turned upside down in a pail of water."

"I know," Miss Pickerell said. "That's because there is a balance between the internal atmospheric pressure and the external water pressure."

"Oh!" the man said, looking impressed.

"The air inside the capsule," Miss Pickerell added, "acts as its own door. It keeps the water out. I just forgot about that for a second."

"Miss Pickerell," Pete broke in quickly, "may I introduce Captain Bean? Captain Bean, this is Miss Pickerell."

Captain Bean stood up, accidentally knocking a framed photograph of two small children, who looked exactly like him, off his desk. Pete bent to pick the picture up. He placed it on a television set that stood against the wall. Miss Pickerell observed that the long narrow room also contained a radio set, a bridge table covered by a neat white cloth, several straight-backed chairs, two red upholstered armchairs, four bunks partially hidden by green curtains, and a galley, complete with stove, sink, and refrigerator. Pots and pans hung on hooks over the

71

sink.   Dishes were neatly stacked on the sink's drainboard.

"I'm sorry, Miss Pickerell," Captain Bean was saying. "I'm . . ."

The abrupt opening of a door near the galley interrupted whatever else Captain Bean was going to say. A man's high voice stormed, "Now, Captain, I have always believed and I believe at this time that . . ."

Before he as much as stepped into the room, Miss Pickerell knew who it was. Not even helium could disguise the identity of Lieutenant Commander S. S. Cripes.

"Good morning, Lieutenant Commander," she said.

Pete stared. Captain Bean looked at her blankly. Lieutenant Commander Cripes smiled.

"Why, if it isn't Miss . . . Miss . . ." he said, with a very pleased expression.

"Miss Pickerell," Captain Bean volunteered.

"Yes, yes, of course," the lieutenant commander said. "The lady with the ocean farm. You mentioned it at breakfast this . . ."

He stopped suddenly. His voice had turned deep again.

"Helium speech converter," Captain Bean said, briefly.

"Fixed," Pete added.

"Thank you," the lieutenant commander answered.

He turned to Miss Pickerell.

"And what brings you here?" he asked.

But again, he didn't seem to expect an answer.

"Lots of things going on that can be solved with a little common sense," he went on. "Now take the personnel problem down here. The men are bored, just looking at fish when they've finished a day's work."

"I don't see how that's possible," Miss Pickerell commented, thoughtfully. "I should think the men would want to study the interesting varieties of fish they see down here."

"Some of the men do that," the lieutenant commander agreed.

"I've made friends with a few of the fish," Captain Bean said. "They wait outside for me to feed them every morning."

Miss Pickerell smiled at Captain Bean.

"There are, however, men who *are* bored," Lieutenant Commander Cripes retorted. "I've ordered television sets, moving-picture projectors, and a circulating-library bookmobile for the entire colony. Now, what do you think of that, Miss Pickerell?"

Miss Pickerell adjusted her glasses, which had begun to slip down her nose.

"Did you say *colony*, Lieutenant Commander?" she asked.

"Twelve installations, so far," the lieutenant commander said, "including living quarters and laboratories for marine chemists, biologists, geologists, geographers, photographers . . ."

"And meteorologists who study ocean currents and the weather," Captain Bean continued. "Also mining engineers who plan how we can dig out uranium and . . ."

"Plus an unmanned vehicle which crawls along on caterpillar tracks on the sea floor," Lieutenant Commander Cripes interrupted to say. "It has television cameras to take pictures of the underwater world and a mechanical arm that can lift rocks, for example, from the ocean floor."

"Plus recording equipment placed on the sea floor," Captain Bean added.

"But none of that need concern you at the moment," the lieutenant commander stated. "Your first business is the problem of your ocean farm."

Miss Pickerell blinked. She hadn't even re-alized that the lieutenant commander knew she had such a problem. He laughed at her amaze-ment.

"Of course, you have a problem with the farm," he said. "Or you probably wouldn't be here. That's common sense, too. And now, some more common sense! I know nothing at all about ocean farms. But I can refer you to someone who does. Top aquaculturalist in the country. When you have a problem, always ask at the top, if you can. Come, Miss Pickerell. I will introduce you to him immediately."

Miss Pickerell gasped. Never in her life had things happened to her so fast. All that infor-mation the lieutenant commander and Captain Bean had been giving her! She was sure she couldn't keep it all in her head. And now! Why, she didn't even know where the lieuten-ant commander was taking her as he led her by the arm to the door near the galley. She de-cided it didn't really matter. Lieutenant Com-mander Cripes was taking her to someone who could help. That was what counted. Without so much as a backward look, she followed him through the doorway.

CHAPTER NINE

Sampling the Ocean Waters

"I'm leaving you with our Dr. Litebody," the lieutenant commander said, as he opened another door and escorted Miss Pickerell into a room that she thought must surely be a laboratory. It had in it an extra-long stainless-steel table, a glass cabinet jammed with bottles, flasks, and test tubes, and several white enamel shelves with more scientific-looking appliances piled on them. A small thin man with white hair stood in front of one of the shelves. He turned around when he heard his name mentioned.

"Yes?" he asked, looking at the lieutenant commander and at Miss Pickerell through horn-rimmed glasses. The lenses on the glasses were very thick and made his lively green eyes seem unusually large.

"I must hurry," the lieutenant commander said to him. "I have to pick up the institute chief from another installation. Miss Pickerell here has a problem with an ocean farm."

He bustled out of the room before Miss Pickerell had a chance even to catch her breath. Dr. Litebody brought two folding chairs from a stack in a corner of the room. He placed them so that he and Miss Pickerell sat facing each other across the table.

"What kind of problem?" he asked quietly.

Miss Pickerell tried to pull her thoughts together. She realized how much depended on her conversation with this aquaculturalist. She came to the point at once.

"The crops on the sea farm are dying," she said briskly. "Using the undersea nuclear reactor to stir up the water only made them get worse."

"Ah!" Dr. Litebody said.

He leaned back in his chair. Miss Pickerell waited for him to say something else.

"A most interesting problem," he commented finally. "There can be many causes."

"Can there?" Miss Pickerell asked, sighing. She had been hoping for too much, she supposed, when she expected Dr. Litebody to have a ready answer for her.

"We must think about the alternatives very carefully," Dr. Litebody went on.

"Yes," Miss Pickerell agreed, wishing Dr.

Litebody would at least mention a few of them.

"Science is sometimes a matter of trial and error," Dr. Litebody said thoughtfully. "The solution may come about almost as an accident. Of course, the trick is to recognize a solution when one sees it coming."

"Naturally," Miss Pickerell replied, trying to be polite but feeling more impatient by the minute.

"On the other hand," Dr. Litebody continued, "science is also a matter of careful reasoning. One examines all possibilities. Then one eliminates some ideas right at the start and follows up on others."

Miss Pickerell brightened. This was more like it.

"Well, we can eliminate everything except the sun and the ocean," she said quickly.

"As far as I know," Dr. Litebody said, smiling a little, "the properties of the sun have not changed lately."

"That leaves the ocean," Miss Pickerell said promptly.

"I should think so," Dr. Litebody replied, taking off his glasses and polishing them while he considered the possibilities, "especially since the water from the deeper ocean stirred up by

the nuclear reactor only made the crops grow worse."

Miss Pickerell jumped up from her chair.

"That means we have to examine the water at the bottom of the ocean," she said, "to find out what's wrong with it."

"*At* and *near* the bottom," Dr. Litebody said, putting his glasses back on. "We have to examine it at varying depths, not only to find out what the trouble is but also just where the trouble comes from."

Miss Pickerell sat down again as a new thought suddenly struck her.

"Should we . . . could we," she asked, "take samples of the water from the varying depths?"

"We certainly should," Dr. Litebody answered. He walked over to the cabinet, looked carefully among its crowded contents, and came back with some steel bottles. They were long and thin and each of them had a thermometer attached to it.

"Nansen bottles!" Miss Pickerell exclaimed. "Euphus uses them. In his advanced biology class."

"Euphus?" Dr. Litebody repeated.

"My middle nephew," Miss Pickerell said.

"Well, to get back to the problem," Dr. Litebody said. "If we entrap some water from varying levels into the Nansen bottles—they have little doors on each end—I can make an examination right here in this laboratory. Since we really have no idea what to look for, I would check on everything—temperature, density, salt content, acidity, dissolved gases, type and quantity of nutrients, type and quantity of other possible properties in the . . ."

"Why, that sounds just right, Dr. Litebody," Miss Pickerell interrupted eagerly. "But how do we get the Nansen bottles lowered into the water? I read somewhere that it could be done with ropes. Who will . . . ?"

"Oh, we use a surface vessel for all that," Dr. Litebody replied. "What we have to do now is to alert the oceanographic institute. Someone there will get in touch with the appropriate vessel. And the required preparations will be made—ropes secured for the lowering of the bottles, assignments made for overseeing the lowering and for recovering the . . ."

Miss Pickerell's heart sank as she listened. The way Dr. Litebody described the procedure, it could take days. Mr. Rugby's farm could be completely ruined by then. No, Miss Pickerell decided, if she was going to help her friend, she would have to think of another, quicker way. There seemed to be only one, really. Miss Pickerell steadied herself as she made up her mind.

"I think it would be best," she said, while she resolutely readjusted her mask, "if I went into the water to collect those samples."

Dr. Litebody unexpectedly whistled.

"You don't really need to do anything like that, Miss Pickerell," he said hastily. "As I explained, we . . ."

"I'd rather," Miss Pickerell said in a firm tone of voice. Then, without giving herself even a moment to change her mind, she reached over and took the bottles from Dr. Litebody.

CHAPTER TEN

Off the Continental Shelf

Holding two Nansen bottles in her right hand and two in her left, Miss Pickerell walked quickly back the way she had come. Dr. Litebody, looking very uneasy, followed closely.

"Miss Pickerell," he protested, "you can't . . . you mustn't go into these waters. They're really not safe."

"Dr. Litebody," Miss Pickerell replied. "You forget that I just came out of these waters. I swam from the elevator to the capsule. It all seemed perfectly safe."

"That was different," Dr. Litebody said. "Mr. Peters was with you."

"I've been undersea before without Mr. Peters," Miss Pickerell told him. "Why, once, I had to swim under a submarine to . . ."

She stopped abruptly. She was wasting too much time.

"Dr. Litebody," she said, standing still for a second so that she could talk directly to him and make her point perfectly clear. "This is an emergency. I'm going into the water to meet that emergency. And nothing terrible has to happen to me."

"Well, no," Dr. Litebody admitted, still looking distressed. "Just don't go too far away from the capsule."

"I won't," Miss Pickerell said, walking on again.

"What I mean," said Dr. Litebody, as he held the door leading to the living quarters open for her, "is that it isn't necessary to go very far. You know, of course, that we are stationed here right near the edge of the continental shelf."

"The edge of the continental shelf," Miss Pickerell repeated, trying hard to control the feeling of butterflies in her stomach.

"Yes," Dr. Litebody said. "The continental shelf is the part of a continent that's under the sea. It slopes out from the land a little, like a shelf that's not quite straight."

"I know about that," Miss Pickerell told him.

"On the average," Dr. Litebody went on, "the continental shelf is about 500 to 600 feet down. We, in the capsule, are roughly about 450 feet down."

"Yes," Miss Pickerell said.

"You'll have to be very careful," Dr. Litebody continued, "because, as I said, we're near the edge of the shelf. If you go past the edge, you could sink down into the deep abyss."

"Forevermore!" Miss Pickerell whispered.

"I beg your pardon?" Dr. Litebody asked.

"Nothing," Miss Pickerell said.

"But since we're already down so deep," Dr. Litebody said reassuringly, "you won't need to go down much farther. I would suggest that you collect water from our level here, from a little above it, and from just a little below. You can do all that without swimming too far away from the capsule."

He took three bottles from Miss Pickerell. Then he labelled one *T* for TOP, one *M* for MIDDLE, and one *B* for BOTTOM with an underwater marker that he had in his breast pocket. Dr. Litebody gave the three bottles to Miss Pickerell. He took the fourth bottle and labelled it *E*.

"For EXTRA," he explained. "In case one of the bottles gets lost. It's always wise to be prepared."

"I understand," Miss Pickerell said, nodding and walking through the door that Dr. Litebody was still holding out for her. "What you want me to do is a kind of vertical collection. I'll remember.

Neither Pete nor Captain Bean was anywhere in sight when Miss Pickerell and Dr. Litebody entered the living quarters. Miss Pickerell thought it was just as well. They might try to keep her back if they knew what she was doing. She walked directly to the hatch.

"Stop, Miss Pickerell! Please stop!" Dr. Litebody, pursuing her, shouted. "You must wear this!"

He picked up a belt from a pile near the hatch and helped Miss Pickerell fasten it around her waist. She saw that it was weighted with lead.

"To give you a slight negative buoyancy," Dr. Litebody explained. "We give you a heavy belt to keep you from coming up too fast."

"But I'm not going down very much farther than this capsule," Miss Pickerell reminded him.

"For every single foot farther down that you go," Dr. Litebody warned, "the pressure of the water pushing on you will increase by approximately one-half pound per square inch. At 450 feet, the pressure is already 235 pounds per square inch, actually."

Miss Pickerell decided that Dr. Litebody was a worrier, quite a lot like Mr. Esticott. She also

86

thought that Dr. Litebody shouldn't be frightening her this way. After all, she had her tank with its automatic regulator to protect her lungs against the water pressure. And she wasn't going very far in any direction. But she really couldn't be angry with Dr. Litebody. She knew he was cautioning her for her own good.

"I'll be careful," she said, as she put the Nansen bottles in a large canvas bag that hung over her shoulder, adjusted the mouthpiece under her mask, climbed down the ladder, and stepped quickly into the water.

Almost immediately, powerful floodlights illuminated the space around her.

"That's nice of Dr. Litebody," Miss Pickerell said to herself. "He didn't want me to be swimming around in the dark. But it isn't really dark. The sun still comes through a little at this depth."

The sunshine was dim though, she had to admit, and she was able to see everything much more clearly with the aid of the floodlights. The first thing she noticed was the condition of the outside of the capsule. It was shamefully dirty.

"If I were Lieutenant Commander Cripes, I'd know what to do with the personnel," she told herself. "I'd start kitchen-patrol duty. Anybody not attending to his work properly would be assigned to scraping off the messy sea-weeds from this capsule. I'll just talk to the lieutenant commander about the idea the next time I see him."

Miss Pickerell made up her mind to collect her first bottleful of water on a level parallel with the capsule, but not too near it. She swam forward. Small fish darted all around her. Bigger fish swam in a leisurely fashion right along with her. They did not seem the least bit afraid. Some of them brushed up against her flippers. One came close and peered into her face mask. Miss Pickerell felt like laughing out loud. She was enjoying this immensely.

She filled the Nansen bottle marked *M*, sealed it by releasing a trigger that pulled down the cover, and decided to ascend.

"This is the hard part," she said, as she kicked her flippers and began to swim upward. The weighted belt slowed her down and made the ascent more gradual. She rose steadily. She passed the sea capsule where she saw that Dr. Litebody was waiting for her near the hatch. She passed three more cigar-shaped capsules that looked exactly like the one she had come from and remembered what the lieutenant commander had said about an underwater colony. Men, huddled around the window of one of the capsules, were staring at her and waving. She waved back. She filled the Nansen bottle marked *T* while she drifted slowly in the water.

Then, pointing her head toward the bottom, she propelled herself downward. This was much easier than going up. The light got dimmer as she went down, but she was able to make out the sea cucumbers moving sluggishly along the shadows and to see a number of lobsters

cautiously backing into their crevices. She swam a little to the left, filled and sealed her third Nansen bottle, and put it back with the others into her canvas bag.

"There!" she said out loud. "It wasn't so difficult after all."

She was just getting ready to swim back to the capsule when she noticed how very near to it she actually was. It occurred to her that she might not have gone down quite far enough.

"Maybe it won't really be a BOTTOM sample from up here," she thought.

She decided to swim down a little deeper. She hadn't broken any of her bottles and she could collect some more water in the extra one.

She began to propel herself down again. Enormous rocks and what appeared to be mountains loomed in the depths below her. They did not look at all friendly. She seemed to be moving toward them much more quickly than she wanted to. Miss Pickerell shuddered. She decided to turn and swim upward. She kicked her flippers again. She tried to drive herself up. She couldn't do it.

"This is ridiculous," she exclaimed, as she rolled over on her side. Kicking as hard as she could, she managed to get her head up on top.

But she kept going down. Faster and faster! She was also beginning to feel very cold and to experience strange and painful sensations in her ears and in her chest.

"There's just not enough air coming in from this tank," she told herself, trying not to panic. "I must think."

She still kept going down, down, down. Her head reeled now with dizziness. Her lungs felt as though they would burst.

"I must be slipping off the shelf," Miss Pickerell panted, as she kept sinking. "I've got to do something . . . something to make myself lighter . . . lighter. . . ."

The second she said the word *lighter,* she knew exactly what she had to do. Using the last bit of her strength, she untied the leaded belt that Dr. Litebody had put around her waist. She shot up from the bottom instantly.

She was going up almost as fast as she had gone down. She was passing the capsule and leaving it behind. She was feeling terrible. She could hardly breathe. There was pressure in her lungs and her head hurt dreadfully. And all she could see were two eels staring at her with hard, unblinking eyes.

Then she saw Pete. He was swimming rapidly toward her. Before she knew it, he had his arms around her and was swimming back with her to the capsule. He placed her in front of him on the first rung of the ladder. Dr. Litebody pulled her up from there.

"The bottles . . ." Miss Pickerell tried to say, as she took one of them out of her bag. She couldn't go on. She started to fall but Dr. Litebody caught her. She lost consciousness.

CHAPTER ELEVEN

The Secret of the Bottles

When Miss Pickerell opened her eyes again, she was lying in one of the bunks behind the green curtains and a strange young man, who introduced himself as the physician on board, was leaning over her. He tested her pulse, listened to her breathing, and, after helping her to get out of her wet diving suit, covered her with a bright plaid blanket.

"You haven't even got the bends," he told her cheerfully. "It's lucky Pete caught you before you could rise high enough to get into real trouble."

"Mercy!" Miss Pickerell said, weakly. "I didn't mean to faint."

"You had a bad fright," the young man said, sympathetically.

"I—I guess so," Miss Pickerell admitted. "I went over the edge of the continental shelf. I didn't expect to do that."

"I don't imagine you did," the young man laughed.

"And I had to take off the leaded belt," Miss Pickerell went on. "I . . ."

"It probably saved your life," the young man interrupted. "But it was an extremely dangerous thing to do. The gases in your body could have expanded rapidly when you shot up and, if Pete hadn't caught you, you would have been very, very sick."

Miss Pickerell shivered as she remembered that terrible moment in the ocean abyss. She tried not to let her mind dwell on it.

"I must talk to Dr. Litebody about the Nansen bottles," she said, sitting up suddenly and feeling her head reel as she did so.

"Dr. Litebody has the bottles," the young man told her, reassuringly. "He's testing the samples in his laboratory right this minute. And now, I think, Miss Pickerell, you'd better get some rest."

"I think so, too," Miss Pickerell said, as she leaned gratefully back against two large pillows. They kept her head up higher than her feet and helped to make the dizziness go away. She was feeling tired and very, very sleepy. From the other side of the green curtains, she could hear the murmur of voices. Lieutenant Commander Cripes was asking questions and Captain Bean and Pete were answering him quietly. Miss Pickerell closed her eyes. The murmur got fainter and fainter. Miss Pickerell slept.

When she awoke, she heard Dr. Litebody talking. She could make out very clearly what he was saying. He was explaining that he had tested the water in all of the bottles.

"And you found?" Lieutenant Commander Cripes asked.

"Nothing abnormal," Dr. Litebody answered. "Absolutely nothing!"

"To a marine biologist," Pete objected, "it just doesn't make sense."

"It certainly doesn't," Miss Pickerell said, sitting up immediately. She still felt a little shaky, but the dizziness was gone and so were the pains in her joints. She dressed quickly and stepped through the curtains.

"Miss Pickerell!" Dr. Litebody, Captain Bean, and Pete all exclaimed at the same time. The lieutenant commander, who was sitting at Captain Bean's desk busily sorting typewritten pages, said, "My dear Miss Pickerell!"

"I heard what you said about the tests, Dr. Litebody," she announced.

"I'm sorry, Miss Pickerell," Dr. Litebody said, looking unhappy.

"There must be something," Miss Pickerell said, sighing. "There must be some reason for the condition of Mr. Rugby's ocean farm."

"I agree," Dr. Litebody said. "But I haven't been able to find it. Come into the laboratory, Miss Pickerell."

Miss Pickerell followed him to the door near the galley and, through it, to the laboratory. The stainless-steel table in the middle of the room was covered with three sets of charts now. Dr. Litebody explained that he had made his notations for each of the bottles on a separate chart. Miss Pickerell noticed that his handwriting was neat and clear. She didn't bother to read the charts. She was sure everything that Dr. Litebody said on them was correct. She walked over to the end of the table where she saw the four bottles she had so recently brought back from the bottom of the ocean. They were standing in a little wooden rack, something like the spice shelf she had in her kitchen on Square Toe Farm.

"I never got a chance to fill the fourth bottle," she said, a little sadly. "I wanted to."

"We had a representative enough sampling," Dr. Litebody replied. "I took water from the top of each of the three full bottles for every test that I made. Salinity, acidity, dissolved gases —everything checked out fine. I couldn't find . . ."

"I know," Miss Pickerell said, picking up the bottle labelled *T* for TOP, and glancing at it idly.

"Oh!" she said, suddenly, as she took a closer look at the bottom.

"What is it, Miss Pickerell?" Dr. Litebody asked instantly.

"I'm not sure yet," Miss Pickerell told him. She put the bottle down, pushed her eyeglasses back more firmly on her nose, picked up the bottle marked *M*, and squinted down into it.

"Mercy!" she said this time. She handed the bottle to Dr. Litebody while she picked up the bottle labelled *B*.

"Miss Pickerell!" Dr. Litebody said now.

"Yes?" Miss Pickerell asked.

"Are you wondering about that green sediment at the bottom of each bottle?" Dr. Litebody asked, sounding very serious.

"I think so," Miss Pickerell replied.

"I hadn't noticed it till now," Dr. Litebody admitted apologetically. "I guess it settled slowly on the bottom after I made the tests." He looked at it carefully. "Whatever it is, it isn't a natural ingredient of ocean water."

"You couldn't have noticed it," Miss Pickerell said. "Not when the bottles were standing in the rack."

"Nevertheless," Dr. Litebody went on, "you are to be congratulated, Miss Pickerell. I will start an analysis of the sediment immediately. Of course, the findings may still be negative, but we won't know until we try."

"Try what?" the voice of Lieutenant Commander Cripes boomed from the doorway.

"An analysis of this GREEN X on the bottom of the bottles," Dr. Litebody said, while he showed it to the lieutenant commander. "Miss Pickerell discovered it."

"That's the spirit, Miss Pickerell," the lieutenant commander said. "Never give up! We may still find something significant there. At the moment, however, we're heading for the surface."

"The surface?" Miss Pickerell asked, not understanding.

The lieutenant commander bustled Miss Pickerell out of the laboratory while he told her that the elevator had arrived at the capsule and that he was accompanying her back to land.

"But why?" Miss Pickerell wanted to know.

"I prefer to wait here and see what Dr. Lite-body . . ."

"Because I'm going up and I refuse to leave you here without me," the lieutenant commander said. "We nearly lost you once, Miss Pickerell. From now on, I'm keeping an eye on you. And that's final!"

He put the tank on her back and adjusted the tubes that went over her shoulders. Pete helped her put on the rubber flippers.

Miss Pickerell thanked Captain Bean and said goodbye. She asked Dr. Litebody if he would give her a little of the GREEN X to take along. Perhaps, she thought, if she kept looking at it and speculating, she might get an idea. Dr. Litebody poured some off from the bottle marked B, for BOTTOM. That bottle had the largest amount of GREEN X. He also promised to keep her and Mr. Rugby informed about any further findings.

Lieutenant Commander Cripes and Pete swam alongside Miss Pickerell as she went the short way from the capsule to the elevator. Inside the elevator, the lieutenant commander said that she had to sit down at once and stay seated. It was a long trip up. He showed her the soft chair he had ordered to be placed for her on the elevator. Miss Pickerell was very grateful. She felt much more tired than she had anticipated. After awhile, she fell asleep. She dreamed that she and Lieutenant Commander Cripes were dashing from one capsule to another asking people what they knew about GREEN X.

It still seemed part of the dream when the lieutenant commander gripped her firmly by the arm and escorted her into another room on the elevator.

"We stay here for awhile now," he said.

"What for?" Miss Pickerell asked, as she looked through the window and saw that they had already surfaced. "We've arrived. I can even see the barge."

"We're not fully decompressed yet," the lieutenant commander explained. "This is a pressurized room where our body systems have a chance to readjust to sea-level conditions."

Miss Pickerell really didn't mind the delay. She was feeling tired again and she took a number of little naps while she waited. Pete offered her something to eat but she wasn't hungry.

The wind revived her when they climbed out of the elevator and onto the barge. She was fully awake by the time she got out of her scuba equipment and into her pink viole dress. But she was still feeling weak and very tired when they approached the landing and she saw that Mr. Rugby and her seven nieces and nephews were standing there.

"My!" she gasped.

"I called them," Mr. Rugby beamed, as he stepped forward to help her off the barge, "the minute Pete telephoned to say you weren't feeling well, Miss Pickerell. I thought they'd be good company for you while you were recuperating, and since it's Saturday and they have no school, I . . ."

"I brought Pumpkins along to comfort you," Rosemary said. "I knew you'd want him."

"And the cow?" Miss Pickerell asked breathlessly.

"Oh, Mr. Kettelson is taking care of her," Euphus said. "She loves him. He keeps talking to her all the time and she listens to every word."

"We rode in her trailer," the twins, Homer and Harry, piped up. "Dwight drove awful fast. We liked that."

Miss Pickerell looked up and down the line of her seven nieces and nephews, from Dwight, the oldest, to the two youngest, who were squealing with delight. How was she ever going to do any thinking with the noise they'd be making, she wondered. Rosemary understood.

"Don't worry about us, Aunt Lavinia," she said. "We're all going swimming. You just take Pumpkins."

Miss Pickerell held out her arms. It felt good to hold his warm furry body and to hear his happy purring.

"Come, Pumpkins," she said. "We'll both of us have some milk. And then we'll lie out in the sunshine for awhile."

Mr. Rugby offered to drive her to the motel immediately. He led the way up the road to the truck.

CHAPTER TWELVE

On the Trail at Last

Miss Pickerell lay stretched out on a gaily-striped green and white beach chair and watched the motel guests enjoying themselves. Some were swimming or splashing around in the water with their children. A few elderly ladies sat on orange campstools under flowered umbrellas and looked appreciatively at the scenery. Personally, Miss Pickerell found it rather flat and monotonous. She said as much to Pumpkins, who evidently agreed with her. He jumped off her lap to wander around a bit. Miss Pickerell didn't worry about him. Before lying down, she had fastened a long cord to his collar. The other end of the cord was securely tied to the leg of her beach chair. Pumpkins couldn't get lost. But Miss Pickerell was beginning to wonder about her nieces and nephews. She sat up to look for them.

Five of them were in sight. Rosemary was helping the two youngest build sand castles. Pumpkins, who had joined them, looked on patiently. As soon as a castle reached some sizeable dimension, he put out a paw and flattened it. The twins were playing tag in the water. They were excellent swimmers. But when Miss Pickerell thought they were going a little too far out, she picked up a small megaphone that Mr. Rugby had left with her and called out to them. Mr. Rugby had also left her a pair of binoculars.

"You can look at the scenery better with binoculars," he had said, before rushing off to join Pete and the lieutenant commander at the institute. Dwight and Euphus had gone with him. Miss Pickerell wished they would come back. She was beginning to feel bored.

It was Pumpkins who first heard the footsteps behind her. He perked up his ears and stared. Miss Pickerell turned to look. Euphus was racing down to her from the motel parking space. Mr. Rugby, panting heavily, followed.

"I did it! I did it, Aunt Lavinia!" Euphus was calling.

"Did what?" Miss Pickerell asked, the minute he came to a standstill in front of her.

"I begged Pete to give me some of that GREEN X stuff you brought back," Euphus said. "From that bottle you asked him to keep safe for you. And I conducted my own experiment."

"Experiment!" Miss Pickerell said, looking from him to Mr. Rugby, who had now caught up and was standing next to Euphus.

"Let me tell you, Aunt Lavinia," Euphus went on, talking so fast that Miss Pickerell had to listen very carefully to understand. "First, I got some healthy algae and some sea water from Pete. I put the water and the algae into three little jars. I called Jar A my control. That's because I changed nothing in Jar A."

"Yes, yes, I know about controls," Miss Pickerell said, briskly.

"I added one drop of the GREEN X to Jar B," Euphus continued. "And I added two drops to Jar C. Then, I waited."

"What happened?" Miss Pickerell asked, holding her breath while he answered.

"Just what I expected," Euphus said. "I looked at the algae in all three jars under Pete's microscope. In Jar A, the algae were still healthy. In Jar B, the algae had lost their green color. In Jar C, the cells had fallen apart. The algae were dead!"

"Mercy!" Miss Pickerell gasped.

"It's true! It's true!" Euphus shouted, jump-

ing up and down in the sand. "Ask anybody."

"It's true," Mr. Rugby said. He was beaming so broadly now, the double chins were beginning to show.

Miss Pickerell sighed. She hated to spoil his pleasure. But she had to tell him. The job of saving his farm was only half over.

"Mr. Rugby . . ." she began.

"Yes, Miss Pickerell?" he asked immediately.

"Mr. Rugby," she said again, "we may know that GREEN X is killing the plants on your farm."

"We certainly do know, Miss Pickerell," Mr. Rugby stated. "Pete said the currents were carrying it up from the bottom of the ocean. That's how my plants got poisoned. Remember, Miss Pickerell, how wilted my plankton were even before Captain Bean used the nuclear reactor to stir the sea?"

"But even if that's how your plants got poisoned," Miss Pickerell said, "we don't know where GREEN X comes from. It's not a natural ingredient of ocean water. Someone is putting it there. If we want to save your farm, Mr. Rugby, we have to find out who is putting the GREEN X into the water and we have to stop him!"

Mr. Rugby stopped beaming.

"I see what you mean, Miss Pickerell," he said.

"Yes," Miss Pickerell said, sighing again.

"Do you have any ideas?" Mr. Rugby asked.

"One," Miss Pickerell said, hesitantly. "It's not a very good one."

"It's better than nothing," Euphus declared, eagerly.

"Well," Miss Pickerell explained, "I was thinking that GREEN X might be some sort of waste that industrial companies were dumping into the ocean. And I was wondering if we could ask . . ."

She stopped to look at Euphus and Mr. Rugby who were listening without saying a word.

"I know," Miss Pickerell said. "There are probably hundreds of places like that to ask in. It's . . . it's not a very practical idea."

"It is, if I organize it properly," Mr. Rugby said, sounding enthusiastic again. "I know every factory for miles around here. I'll make up a map. I'll send Dwight in one direction, Pete in another, and . . . Why, even Lieutenant Commander Cripes will probably want to go, Miss Pickerell. There's no telling what we'll come up with. Please excuse us, Miss Pickerell. I think Euphus and I should get back now."

"Yes, sir!" Euphus said, as he ran up the hill with Mr. Rugby.

Miss Pickerell saw them climb into the truck and ride off in the direction of the institute.

"I still don't think it's a very good idea," she said to herself.

She turned back and looked at the beach again. The sun had gone down behind a cloud. The elderly ladies were folding up their campstools and making their way to the motel lounge. The swimmers had left the ocean. Only a few children, Homer and Harry among them, were still splashing around its edges. Rosemary was watching them.

"I've got to think," Miss Pickerell told herself, as she lay back in the beach chair and looked out at the ocean. There was only a motor launch on its surface now. Miss Pickerell studied it curiously. It was unusually big and dirty and it chugged along at a fairly rapid pace. It was doing something else too, something very strange.

Miss Pickerell stood up quickly and peered out at the launch. She was almost positive that a man on the launch was emptying something out of a barrel and into the ocean. She picked up the binoculars from where Mr. Rugby had placed them alongside her chair. She looked again. Now, she could see the launch as clearly as if it were right on the beach with her. She could see that there were two men emptying barrels out into the ocean. She could see that what was coming out of the barrels was a thick, oozy substance. It was definitely and unmistakably green.

Miss Pickerell kept on looking. The launch

was moving farther and farther away from the shoreline and the men were emptying barrel after barrel into the water's depths. Miss Pickerell watched until she could see only an outline in the distance.

"Well," she said to herself, as she sat down again. "What do I do now?"

CHAPTER THIRTEEN

Action! Action!

In Miss Pickerell's mind, the question almost answered itself. As soon as she saw the launch turn around and head for the shore, she knew what she had to do.

"I must follow it," she told herself. "I'm sure it's going to move along the shoreline back to its home base. And that's where the GREEN X must come from. Now, we'll have action!"

She leaped to her feet. Stopping only to ask Rosemary to be sure and keep an eye on Pumpkins, she ran up the slope. In an instant, she was at the wheel of her automobile. The trailer was still attached to it. Miss Pickerell didn't bother to have the trailer unhitched. She wanted to be ready the minute the motor launch made an important move.

She didn't have to wait long. The launch was chugging back into full sight. As it came closer, it turned to the right and began to travel along the shoreline in a northerly direction.

111

Miss Pickerell drove immediately to the north-bound lane of the adjacent highway.

For awhile, only the white and red road guards separated the lane from the ocean. Miss Pickerell and the launch proceeded in almost a parallel line.

But in a few minutes, the road began to wind. First, a large clump of trees separated Miss Pickerell from the ocean. She saw the launch again, though, after she left the trees behind. Then, a lot of prefabricated summer houses got in the way. For about a mile, Miss Pickerell drove without being able to see the ocean at all. The road turned right, at last, sharply back in the direction of the ocean. Miss Pickerell couldn't see the launch yet. But she could hear its chugging in the still afternoon air.

When the road began to parallel the ocean again, she saw that the launch was considerably ahead of her. She put her foot on the gas pedal to bring up her speed. The old car squeaked as it rattled along. And the empty trailer in the rear clattered so much, Miss Pickerell was half afraid it might fall off. She sighed. She wished she had thought of calling the Governor. He could have come with his helicopter. Following the launch would have been so easy with a helicopter. Miss Pickerell tucked a loose hair-pin into place. She drove doggedly on.

Then, suddenly, the launch began to slow down. It was making its way to a group of gray weatherbeaten buildings that stood facing the ocean, only a few feet inland. Miss Pickerell turned off the highway and around, first to the back and then to the ocean side of the buildings.

They looked completely deserted. The windows were shuttered, with red rust on their hinges. The doors were bolted and barred. There were no signs anywhere to show who owned the buildings, or what, if anything, went on inside. Miss Pickerell didn't take the time to think about this. She was too busy concentrating on the barrels of green waste piled up in front.

"Dozens of them!" she breathed. "I must get this information to the oceanographic institute."

She drove quickly back to the highway. Before going on, she took a good look around. She wanted to be sure she would find the place again. On her right was a billboard announcing that the Hideaway Hotel was only one mile up. On her left was, of course, the ocean.

"I'll remember now," she told herself.

She paused to take one last look. The launch had stopped. Two men in brown leather jackets and checked caps on their heads were getting off. They moved directly to the barrels and began carting them, one at a time, onto the launch.

"They just can't go on," Miss Pickerell exclaimed in exasperation. "I must tell them how dangerous it is."

She drove around to the front of the building.

"Yoo hoo!" she called out to them.

The two men looked up. The taller of the two, who was also very stout, asked, "What is it, lady?"

"My name is Miss Pickerell," she told him.

"We got work to do, Miss Pickerell," the other man said. "Don't you see you're interrupting?"

"That's just it," Miss Pickerell answered. "You have to stop doing that work. You have to stop right this minute."

"Not when we're getting time-and-a-half overtime pay, we don't," the first man said, hauling a barrel up over his head.

"No! No!" Miss Pickerell called. "You're polluting the . . ."

The man neither listened nor stopped what
he was doing. He carried the barrel full of
GREEN X onto the launch and came back for
another.

"You don't understand," Miss Pickerell told both men who were stooping down to pick up some more cases.

"Don't understand what?" the second man said, straightening up and pushing his cap back on his head. Miss Pickerell noticed that he was bald.

"You're poisoning the plants," she started to say. "Maybe even the fish who eat the ocean plants and then the people who eat the . . ."

"Aw, shucks!" the stout man interrupted. "We got no time to listen to crazy stories."

"Crazy stories!" Miss Pickerell spluttered. "Why, if you saw my friend Mr. Rugby's ocean farm, you'd know what I was talking about. You'd see how withered the crops are and . . ."

"Never heard of ocean farms," the bald-headed man broke in.

He groaned as he picked up a particularly heavy barrel.

"Are you trying to tell us, lady," the stout man asked, "that this stuff is spoiling some ocean farm? Well, I never heard of ocean farms, either. But I can tell you one thing for sure. You can't prove it."

"I can," Miss Pickerell answered, feeling as

though she was going to explode. "I can and I will!"

"Aw, shucks!" the man said again.

Miss Pickerell was practically livid with indignation. Her hands shook as she steered the car back on the highway.

"I'll be back," she told herself. "I'll be back and I'll bring the Governor. He'll make them stop quickly enough."

But even while she was saying these comforting words, she knew that the big stout man was right. She had no proof that this green substance was poisoning Mr. Rugby's crops. And if she didn't find proof, the dumping would go on and poison more plants and fish and people . . .

Miss Pickerell forced herself to push these terrible thoughts out of her head. She began to think instead of ways of providing proof. There was a way, she was sure. Somewhere in the back of her mind, she knew just what that way was. It was something she had to remember. But she couldn't. Once, the idea was almost on the tip of her tongue. Then the memory was gone. It nagged at her all the way back to the institute.

CHAPTER FOURTEEN

Miss Pickerell Has an Idea

The door to the oceanographic institute was open. Mr. Rugby, his elbows resting on a small telephone table, his chin sunk on his hands, sat in the entrance-way. Miss Pickerell took one look at his flushed, unhappy face and, almost immediately, the idea that had been escaping her began to take shape in her mind. She nearly laughed with relief. It was such a simple idea. And it could solve all their problems.

"Mr. Rugby . . ." she began, taking a deep breath so that she could tell him everything without stopping. But Mr. Rugby spoke first.

"Hopeless!" he said, heaving an enormous sigh.

Miss Pickerell sat down opposite him.

"Things may not be as bad as they seem, Mr. Rugby," she began again.

"Thank you for trying to encourage me," Mr. Rugby replied. "I appreciate your friendship. But I feel very sad. I . . ."

He stopped to answer the telephone.

"Yes, Lieutenant Commander," he said. "I'm still minding the telephone, just the way you told me to. Yes, everyone's been calling in. Not a clue so far. Not even a . . ."

"Let me speak to him, Mr. Rugby, please," Miss Pickerell said, taking the telephone out of his hands.

"Certainly," Mr. Rugby said, but Miss Pickerell was already talking.

"I think I have found the place where the GREEN X comes from," she was saying. "It's in front of some locked-up buildings near the Hideaway Hotel."

"Those are abandoned warehouses," Mr. Rugby burst out. "And the Hideaway Hotel isn't a hideaway at all. It's right on the main road."

"Thank you, Lieutenant Commander," Miss Pickerell went on. "That's my idea exactly. I'll expect you here in five minutes."

Miss Pickerell hung up the receiver. She looked up at Mr. Rugby, who was staring at her blankly.

"Listen, Mr. Rugby," she said, "I saw two men dumping green waste into the ocean. Now, if we can prove that this is the same GREEN X that we found in the Nansen bottles, we will know who is ruining your ocean farm. And I have an idea about how we can do that."

"You have?" Mr. Rugby repeated.

"Yes," Miss Pickerell said. "Do you have a paper and pencil handy?"

"Why, yes, Miss Pickerell," he said, handing both to her. "I've had these ready all evening, in case the clues should start coming in. But . . ."

"Sometimes I think better when I make an outline," Miss Pickerell said, as she wrote carefully on the yellow pad of paper that Mr. Rugby gave her. He stood up and walked behind her so that he could look over her shoulder while she was writing. He read every sentence aloud:

Plan for Providing Proof

1. Get back to the warehouse immediately. (The lieutenant commander said that, too.)
2. Take along some radioactive material. (How? A jar? A bottle? I'll ask the lieutenant commander.)
3. Get the radioactive material into the green waste in one or two of the barrels. (I think there will still be some barrels full of the green waste near the warehouse. The men

couldn't have dumped all of them today. There wasn't time.)

4. The GREEN X in these barrels (if it is GREEN X) will now be tagged with radioactivity.

5. Tomorrow, after the men have dumped these barrels, we will search the water near Mr. Rugby's ocean farm.

6. If the tagged samples have gone in the direction of the farm, we will find them with the Geiger counters. (That should be easy because Geiger counters detect radiation and show it. And we will be proving that the green waste comes up with the ocean currents to Mr. Rugby's farm.)

7. I think we should also take a little of the waste material back with us and have the chemist at the oceanographic institute check to see if it is the same as our own GREEN X. (He can compare it with the GREEN X in my bottle. THIS WILL BE THE FINAL PROOF.)

8. Our next step is to stop this dreadful and dangerous pollution!!

Miss Pickerell was just placing a period at the end of her last sentence when Lieutenant Commander Cripes and Pete walked in. Miss Pickerell handed them the outline.

The lieutenant commander gasped twice while he was reading it. Pete, who finished first, looked in a startled way at Miss Pickerell.

"Whew!" Pete exclaimed.

"Splendid!" the lieutenant commander added. "How did you think it all out, Miss Pickerell?"

"It's not all my own idea," Miss Pickerell said, modestly. "I learned about the Geiger counter from a sheriff once. He had the measles and he looked terribly worried. I remembered it when I walked into the institute and saw Mr. Rugby's face. He looked red and worried, too."

"Well, that was a good start," the lieutenant commander said, laughing out loud. "And you have a capital plan there, Miss Pickerell."

He looked at the outline again.

"In answer to your question under item #2," he said, "we will, of course, use radioactive material that comes in long tubes. We can push these tubes into the barrels and . . . But that's neither here nor there at this moment. We have no time to waste. Pete!"

"I know what to do," Pete said. "I'll meet you out in front."

He ran down the corridor. The lieutenant commander, still holding Miss Pickerell's outline, led the way out of the institute. They were just getting into the front of Mr. Rugby's truck when Pete raced toward them. He was carrying a lead cylinder with the tube of radio-active material in it in one hand and a pair of tongs attached to a long handle in the other. As a protection against radiation, he wore a lead jacket and a pair of lead gloves. He climbed carefully into the back of the truck. Mr. Rugby pressed down on the gas pedal.

"I know the way," he said, as he began to speed.

Miss Pickerell didn't say anything. She was feeling much too worried to talk. She was only hoping that there would be some barrels full of the green waste in front of the warehouse. What if there weren't? What if the two men had finished their dumping job for the day? What if there were only empty barrels by the time she and Pete and Mr. Rugby and the lieutenant commander got there? What would they do then?

She had no chance to go on with her questions. The truck was approaching the warehouse. The headlights picked out the shuttered windows, the bolted doors, and the covered barrels standing in front. There were at least twelve of them.

Pete jumped out of the truck just as Mr. Rugby jammed on the brakes. Miss Pickerell, the lieutenant commander, and Mr. Rugby followed. The lieutenant commander held Pete's flashlight while Mr. Rugby opened the first barrel, the second, the third, the fourth. All were full of the green waste.

"Quick!" the lieutenant commander whispered. "Before somebody sees us."

Pete carefully slid the tube out of the cylinder that covered it. He held the tongs out in front of him. With one swift gesture, he lifted the tube with the tongs and thrust it into the waste in the first barrel. Everyone let out a sigh of relief.

"That's enough," the lieutenant commander ordered. "One barrel will give us what we need."

"We wait about five minutes now," Pete said, looking at his watch. "We have to give the radioactive material a chance to tag the green waste."

"I'll keep track of the time," the lieutenant commander stated.

"We need a sample to take back with us," Miss Pickerell told Pete. "For the chemist."

"I haven't forgotten," Pete said, as he

scooped up some of the waste material from the second barrel and transferred it into a jar that he took out of his pocket. He gave Miss Pickerell the jar to hold.

"Five minutes!" the lieutenant commander announced. "You can take the tube out now, Pete."

Pete did so immediately. He used the tongs to replace the tube in the cylinder. Mr. R. replaced the lids on all the barrels and then checked to make certain that they were on.

"Fine!" the lieutenant commander said. "From now on, it will all proceed like clockwork. Without a hitch, I assure you, Miss Pickerell."

On the way back, he announced that he would get up early the next day to watch the dumping of the barrels from the launch. Then, he would organize the Geiger-counter search. Miss Pickerell didn't remind him that the next day was Sunday and the men might not be working. She was too tired to think about it. She was also concerned about the children. It was long past their supper hour. She hoped they had had the sense not to wait for her. She hoped, too, that Rosemary had remembered to feed Pumpkins.

CHAPTER FIFTEEN

The Proof

The desk clerk gave Miss Pickerell her wake-up call, just as she had asked him to, at 6:30 the next morning. He also told her that he had a message for her from Lieutenant Commander Cripes. The lieutenant commander had telephoned at 6 o'clock to give Miss Pickerell some news. The desk clerk had written it all down.

"Every word, Miss Pickerell," he said. "Just the way the lieutenant commander gave it to me. He insisted on that."

"Thank you," Miss Pickerell said. "Please read the message."

"Yes, ma'm," the desk clerk said.

He read: "Mr. Rugby and I went to the Hideaway Hotel, which we used as an observation post, at 5:30 this morning. It wasn't a moment too soon. The two men were already in front of the warehouse."

"They're probably getting paid double time on a Sunday," Miss Pickerell said.

"I beg your pardon?" the desk clerk asked.

"Nothing," Miss Pickerell replied. "Please go on."

He continued to read: "The barrel with the radioactive waste was the third one they picked up. I could see it clearly through my field glasses. I saw, too, the exact place where they dumped the waste into the ocean from their launch.

Lieutenant Commander S.S. Cripes, U.S. Navy, Retired"

Miss Pickerell thanked the desk clerk and sat down to think about what she should do. It would take a few hours for the waste to drift up to Mr. Rugby's farm—if, indeed, it drifted up there at all. She felt far too impatient just to sit around and wait. She dressed hurriedly and fed Pumpkins some of the canned meat that Rosemary had brought along for him. He looked at her reproachfully.

"I know," Miss Pickerell told him. "You had the same thing for supper last night and it's not your favorite food. But you have to eat *something*."

Pumpkins understood. He ate all of his breakfast. Afterward, he jumped up on the broad window sill, gave himself his usual face wash, and settled down to watch the passing birds. Miss Pickerell made sure that the screen in the window was securely fastened. Then she left a note for Rosemary, had a large glass of milk in the dining room, and started out to walk to the sea farm.

Miss Pickerell liked walking and this walk took her across pleasant countryside and through part of the town of Bothomley. No one else seemed to be up and out so early in the morning. Miss Pickerell could hear her own footsteps as she passed the fine shops on the main street. She stopped for a moment to take another look at the Sea Shack. By pressing her nose against the side door where the green blind left a little space, she was able to get a glimpse of the inside. She saw a bright red wallpaper, the fringe of a matching table-cloth, and part of a picture that looked familiar. She wasn't sure but she had an idea that it might be a picture of herself. She recognized her big, black umbrella.

Miss Pickerell walked on. At the end of the main street, she began to climb the hill where Mr. Rugby had taken her when he first drove her from the station to the ocean farm. The thoughts raced through her mind as she walked. Where was the radioactive green waste now? Was it drifting up to Mr. Rugby's plants? Was it, perhaps, already mixing with the waters there? Most important of all, was it *really* the same as GREEN X?

Miss Pickerell walked faster and faster. After she passed the top of the hill, she began to run. She saw the ocean in front of her. She saw the ocean farm. She saw Dwight and Euphus and Homer and Harry and Pete and Mr. Rugby standing on the dock. As she got nearer, she saw that they were all grouped around the lieutenant commander and that everybody had earphones on and was carrying a Geiger counter.

The lieutenant commander stepped forward to meet her.

"We're planning our strategy," he said.

"We haven't heard any clicks so far," Homer said.

"We've tried everywhere," Harry said. "Near the seaweeds, near the rockweeds, in the kelp beds, among the diatoms . . ."

"Oh!" Miss Pickerell said.

"I have something important to tell you, Miss Pickerell," the lieutenant commander said. "The chemist's report is positive. What I mean is that his analysis showed that the green waste is *exactly* the same as our GREEN X."

Miss Pickerell's spirits rose. Then, immediately, they sank again. What good was the analysis if they couldn't prove that the green waste was coming up from the dumping place to Mr. Rugby's farm? She walked over to where the two rowboats lay anchored.

"I must think," she told herself, as she carefully reviewed what they had already accomplished. They knew now that the green waste was the same as GREEN X, that it was, as Euphus had proven, a dangerous killer of ocean life, that it could . . . A brand new idea suddenly popped into her head.

"Lieutenant Commander!" she called.

"Yes?" he asked, joining her.

She looked at her watch. It was 8:15 exactly.

"Lieutenant Commander," she said, "according to your estimates, the green waste should have been here by now. It is *not* here. Where has it gone?"

"I wish I knew," the lieutenant commander sighed.

"But that's just the point," Miss Pickerell went on. "We can easily find out. Do you remember the spot where the launch dumped the radioactive green waste this morning?"

"Of course, I remember," the lieutenant commander replied.

"Well," Miss Pickerell explained, "I suggest that we row out to that spot. We'll be sure to hear the clicking there. And we'll keep following the clicks with our Geiger counters. We'll trace . . ."

"Admirable!" the lieutenant commander exclaimed.

"May I row? May I row?" Euphus begged.

"Yes," Miss Pickerell told him. "As fast as you can."

Euphus jumped into the nearer of the two rowboats. Lieutenant Commander Cripes helped Miss Pickerell get in. Then he untied the boat and joined her on the seat facing Euphus.

"Due west, Euphus," he said. "Due west!"

"Yes, sir," Euphus replied, dipping the oars in the water and steering in the direction the lieutenant commander had indicated.

"I will use my Geiger counter," the lieutenant commander went on, talking to Miss Pickerell now, "and you can use Euphus's."

"Yes," Miss Pickerell said, taking the Geiger counter he handed her.

"Now to the left a little, Euphus," the lieutenant commander ordered. "That's fine. We'll soon be there."

Miss Pickerell put the long cord with the Geiger-counter earphones attached to it around her neck, examined the little black box to make sure that all the cords were connected, and picked up a glass-and-metal tube.

"You know all about using the Geiger counter, I imagine, Miss Pickerell," the lieutenant commander said, smiling.

"I know how to use it on land," Miss Pickerell replied. "I assume it's more or less the same in the water."

"Right!" the lieutenant commander said. "The tubes are our probes. We let them dangle in the water. When they detect radiation, we hear the clicks in the earphones."

"Shall we begin now, Lieutenant Commander?" Miss Pickerell asked.

The lieutenant commander took a long look around him. He seemed to be measuring distances.

"I believe we're approaching the spot now," he said.

Miss Pickerell nodded. She lowered her probe over her side of the rowboat and adjusted her earphones. The lieutenant commander did the same. Euphus continued to row.

Almost immediately, she heard the clicks. But they were slow and very irregular. They

were only background sounds. She had once heard Euphus say that such background sounds were created by the constant bombardment of particles from outer space, maybe even by cosmic rays.

Miss Pickerell was trying to figure this out when she heard the clicks coming more rapidly. She looked at the lieutenant commander. He was smiling broadly and motioning for Euphus to pull hard at the oars.

The clicks continued to come, more and more rapidly and more and more distinctly. In Miss Pickerell's ears, they were beginning to sound like a volley of machine-gun shots.

"This is it!" the lieutenant commander

shouted. "This is the spot where they dumped the radioactive waste."

Miss Pickerell couldn't hear him with the earphones on. But she knew what he was saying. She nodded vigorously. The lieutenant commander ordered Euphus to keep rowing.

But the clicks got fainter and fainter as they went on. Then, they stopped altogether.

"I know," Miss Pickerell said, excitedly motioning for the lieutenant commander to take off his earphones. "The waste didn't go beyond this point. It went the other way, back toward Mr. Rugby's farm."

"We heard no clicks on the farm," the lieutenant commander objected.

"We were probably too early," Miss Pickerell said. "The radioactive waste may be drifting back there right now."

The lieutenant commander nodded this time.

"We'll begin by retracing our steps," he said to Euphus. "Turn the boat around."

Euphus made a sharp U turn. Miss Pickerell and Lieutenant Commander Cripes readjusted their earphones. Both of them grinned when they heard the clicks again.

"Now, we'll follow the clicks," the lieutenant commander told Euphus. "I'll keep calling out to you which way to row."

They proceeded in zigzag fashion, now to the right a little, now to the left, now more to the left, now back to the right. The clicks led them in this uneven manner all the way back to the farm.

And when they approached the dock, they heard the jubilant shouts from the searchers on the farm. The clicks had been registering on the Geiger counters there, too.

"GREEN X has penetrated the entire area," the lieutenant commander said. "Congratulations, Miss Pickerell. You have proved it all."

"I must go and call the Governor," Miss Pickerell answered, as she leaned on the hand that Mr. Rugby was extending to her and stepped out of the boat.

CHAPTER SIXTEEN

Euphus Makes a Decision

Mr. Rugby insisted on making a party in Miss Pickerell's honor. He planned it for six o'clock that evening at the Sea Shack. He invited everyone he could think of and everyone came, including the Governor.

Mr. Kettelson arrived first. He came in young Mr. Gilhuly's Rural Free Delivery truck. Mr. Gilhuly drove. Mr. Kettelson sat in the back with Miss Pickerell's cow.

"I just can't bear to be separated from her," Mr. Kettelson commented.

Miss Pickerell said that she understood. She saw to it that the cow was immediately put in her trailer where she would be more comfortable.

Several newspaper and television reporters took pictures of Miss Pickerell as she was leading her cow from the mail truck to the trailer. One reporter who had overheard Mr. Kettelson's conversation insisted on a picture of him with the cow. Both Miss Pickerell and Mr. Kettelson made sure that the trailer was parked where they could keep an eye on it from the window of the restaurant.

Mr. Esticott arrived shortly after Mr. Kettelson. He looked very crestfallen. He raced over to Miss Pickerell who was standing near her cow.

"I was wrong," he said at once. "I was wrong about everything."

"You were right about the encyclopedia," Miss Pickerell told him. "I'm ordering up-to-date supplements to——"

A helicopter noisily circling overhead interrupted whatever else Miss Pickerell was going to say. It landed on the front lawn of the dry goods store with the yellow shutters, diagonally across the road from the Sea Shack. The Governor, wearing gray suede gloves and carrying a cane in one hand and a corsage of American Beauty roses in the other, emerged from the helicopter. He was quickly followed by a number of important-looking men, also wearing gloves and carrying canes, and by the lady reporter from the SQUARE TOE GAZETTE who had on her big straw picture hat. The hat was flapping a little in the wind.

The lady reporter helped the Governor pin the corsage of flowers on Miss Pickerell's pink dress, right below her left shoulder. The Governor introduced the men who were with him. Four of them were state anti-pollution experts. The fifth man was a member of the President's Science Advisory Committee. He and the Governor led the way into the restaurant. Everyone had to be very careful walking in because of the television wires on the floor.

Mr. Rugby was in charge of the seating arrangements. He escorted Miss Pickerell to the middle of a long table, covered with a pink crepe paper tablecloth and decorated with gingerbread figures of sea cows. He placed the Governor, the lady reporter, the member of the President's Science Advisory Committee, and the anti-pollution experts on Miss Pickerell's right. Her seven nephews and nieces, beginning with Dwight, the oldest, and going right on down to the two youngest, and next to them, their parents, sat on her left. Rosemary held Pumpkins on her lap.

The other tables in the room were rapidly filling up. Miss Pickerell, peering over a battery of microphones which someone had placed directly in front of her, saw almost everybody she knew. She wondered how Mr. Rugby had ever found the time to get them all together.

When everybody was seated, Mr. Rugby stepped up to the microphones. The television cameras went into action instantly. Mr. Rugby said that this was the most important moment of his whole life so far and that he owed it all to Miss Pickerell. Eventually, when he had his sea recipes in shape again, he would name one of his new dishes "The Miss Pickerell Special."

Miss Pickerell smiled. Mr. Rugby went on to say, "I now introduce to you Lieutenant Commander S. S. Cripes, U.S. Navy, Retired."

The lieutenant commander was in white dress-uniform and was wearing all his ribbons and medals for the occasion. He saluted briskly when he stood in front of the microphones and the whirring television cameras. He then said that he was here as a representative of the Oceanographic Institute. It was his privilege to award to Miss Pickerell, in recognition of the help she had given to the science of oceanography, "the Order of the Dolphin Wings." He turned aside to face Miss Pickerell. He stooped low to kiss her hand. Every reporter in the room ran forward. Every camera clicked. The lady reporter, who had no camera, rushed over to Miss Pickerell to help her pin the Dolphin Wings on, right next to her corsage.

The applause was deafening. In the middle of it, Mr. Rugby introduced the Governor. Everyone stood up and went right on applauding.

The Governor, bowing and smiling, waved for them to sit down.

"Lieutenant Commander Cripes," he began, "has mentioned Miss Pickerell's help to the science of oceanography. But he didn't spell it out for you. Let me do that now."

The Governor paused. He stroked his moustache solemnly. The room was hushed.

"Let me tell you two startling facts," the Governor went on. "Fact #1: There are approximately 30 million more people in the world every year than the year before. By

A.D. 2,000, it is estimated that the world's population will be more than double what it is today. Fact #2: The land alone cannot keep up with the increasing demand for food. Man must look to the sea. Man must farm the sea and develop ways for gathering ever larger and better sea harvests. This is what our good friend, Mr. Rugby, has been trying to do. Mr. Rugby nearly failed. He would have failed if Miss Pickerell had not stepped in to track down the poison that was destroying his ocean farm."

The Governor stopped to take a drink of

water. Mr. Rugby rushed over to the microphones. But the Governor hadn't finished talking. Mr. Rugby galloped right back. Miss Pickerell thought about Euphus's science teacher. Both men had talked about the great importance of ocean farming in almost the same way.

"In tracking down the harmful substance that was polluting Mr. Rugby's farm," the Governor continued, "Miss Pickerell has saved not only his farm but indirectly every other pioneering ocean farm in the country. In this state, my anti-pollution specialists and I have already taken steps to prevent such pollution anywhere. I have so advised the member of the President's Science Advisory Committee who will speak to you now."

The applause was so loud, the member of the President's Science Advisory Committee had to begin his speech three times before he could be heard. The clapping got even louder when he suggested that the President's job would probably be a lot easier if there were more Miss Pickerells around and when he announced that he, personally, was nominating Miss Pickerell for honorary membership on his committee.

Mr. Rugby ran forward to shake Miss Pickerell's hand. He also gave her a pink paper napkin with a note written on it. Miss Pickerell read the note quickly. She folded the napkin up the minute the member of the President's Science Advisory Committee began to talk again.

"Your Governor has already given you the facts," he said. "I will add to them by saying that ocean farms can offer us a harvest of food that may be far greater than anything we can grow on land. I will also say that our very survival in this world may indeed depend on how well we cultivate our oceans. Your own courageous Miss Pickerell has helped us move in this direction."

It was Miss Pickerell's turn to speak. Mr. Rugby shouted this over the microphones. Miss Pickerell got up slowly. She didn't know exactly what to say. But the words came to her when she looked around at all the friendly faces.

"I had help," she said, gravely. "I had help from Pete and Dr. Litebody and Captain Bean and the lieutenant commander and even from my oldest niece, Rosemary, who minded my cat, Pumpkins, while I followed the dumping launch. And I had the help of my middle nephew, Euphus, who actually conducted the experiment which proved that GREEN X poisoned sea plants. Please stand up, Euphus."

Euphus did so. Every camera in the room focused on him.

Miss Pickerell unfolded the pink paper napkin that she held in her hand. She lowered her glasses on her nose so that she could read over them.

"I have here a note from my middle nephew, Euphus," she said. "He writes, I HAVE TO TELL MY SCHOOL GUIDANCE COUN-SELOR NEXT WEEK WHAT I WANT TO BE WHEN I GROW UP. I HAVE DECIDED TO BECOME AN OCEANOGRAPHER. WHAT DO YOU THINK?"

Miss Pickerell pushed up her glasses and took a deep breath.

"My answer to Euphus," she said, "is that I can think of nothing more important than work that will help feed a hungry world."

Miss Pickerell sat down. Everybody else stood up. Everybody clapped and clapped except the lady reporter. She was too busy drying her eyes with her big lace handkerchief.